SIR LADYBUG

and the
BOOKWORMS

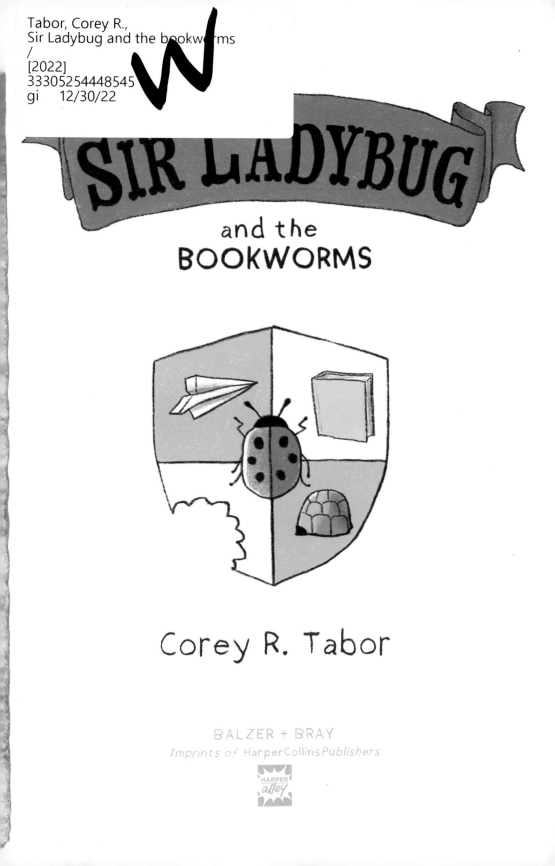

Corey R. Tabor

BALZER + BRAY
Imprints of HarperCollins Publishers

HARPER
alley

Balzer + Bray is an imprint of HarperCollins Publishers.

HarperAlley is an imprint of HarperCollins Publishers.

Sir Ladybug and the Bookworms
Copyright © 2022 by Corey R. Tabor
All rights reserved. Manufactured in Italy.
Library of Congress Control Number: 2022934019
ISBN 978-0-06-306912-1

The art for this book was created digitally.
Typography by Dana Fritts and Corey R. Tabor
22 23 24 25 26   RTLO   10 9 8 7 6 5 4 3 2 1
❖
First Edition

CONTENTS

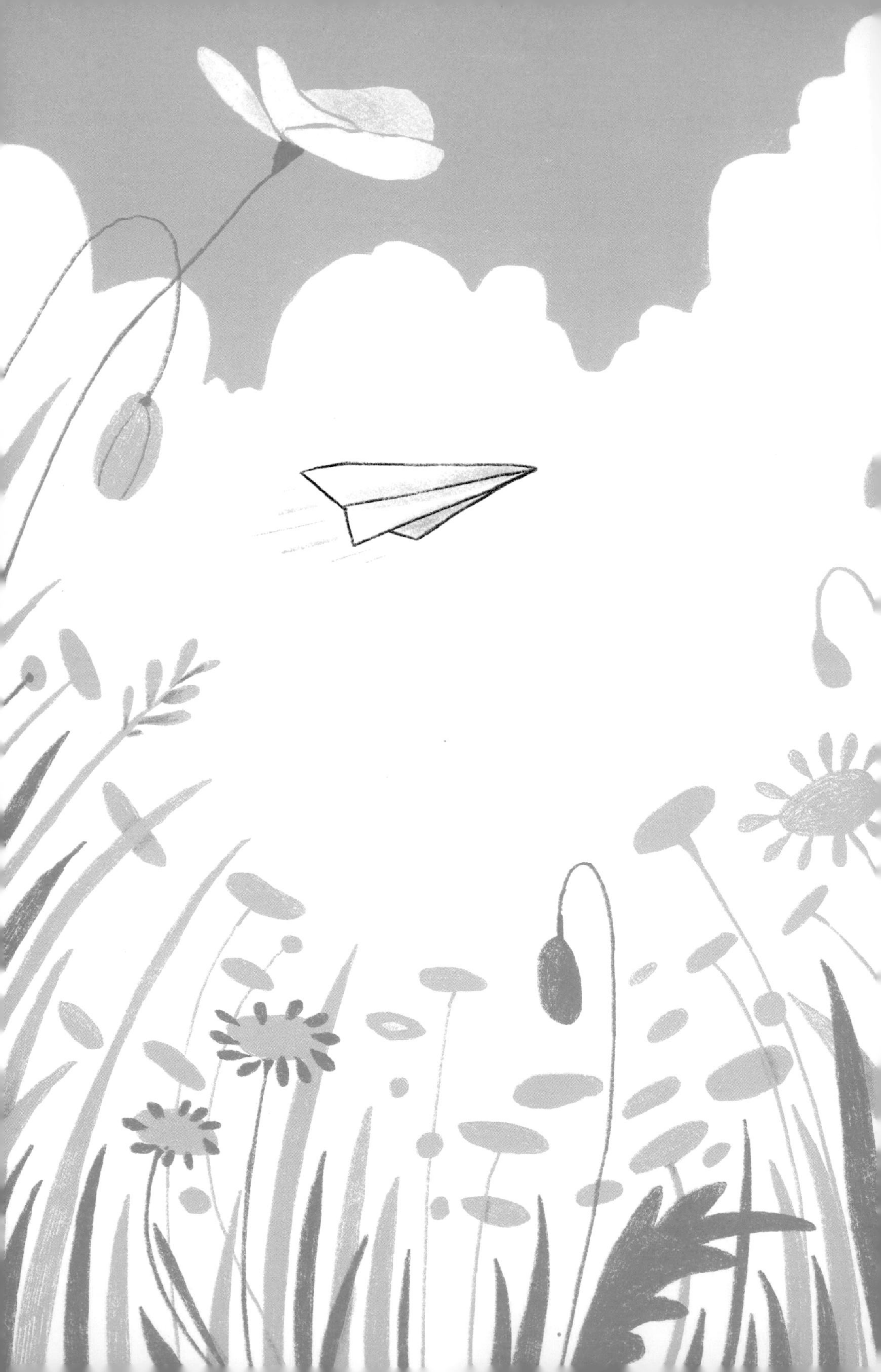

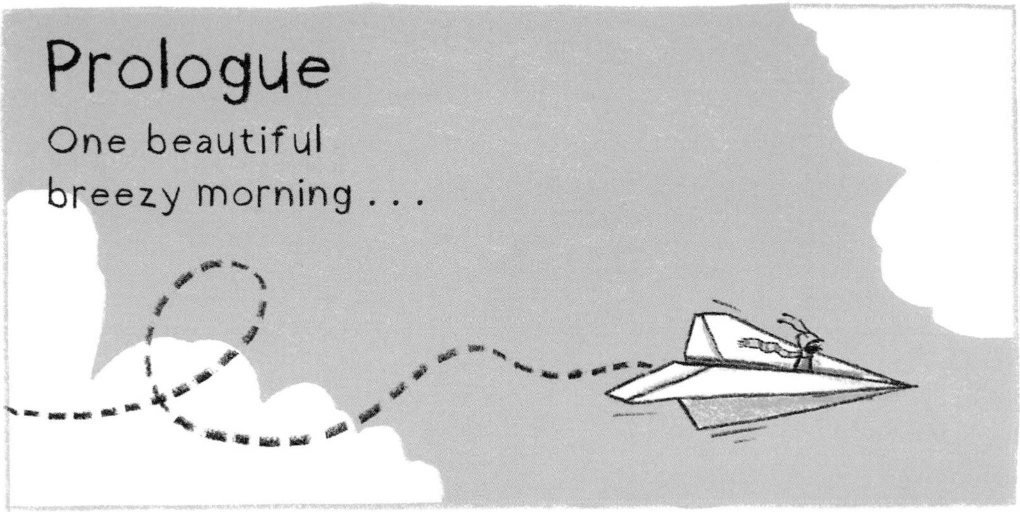
Prologue
One beautiful breezy morning . . .

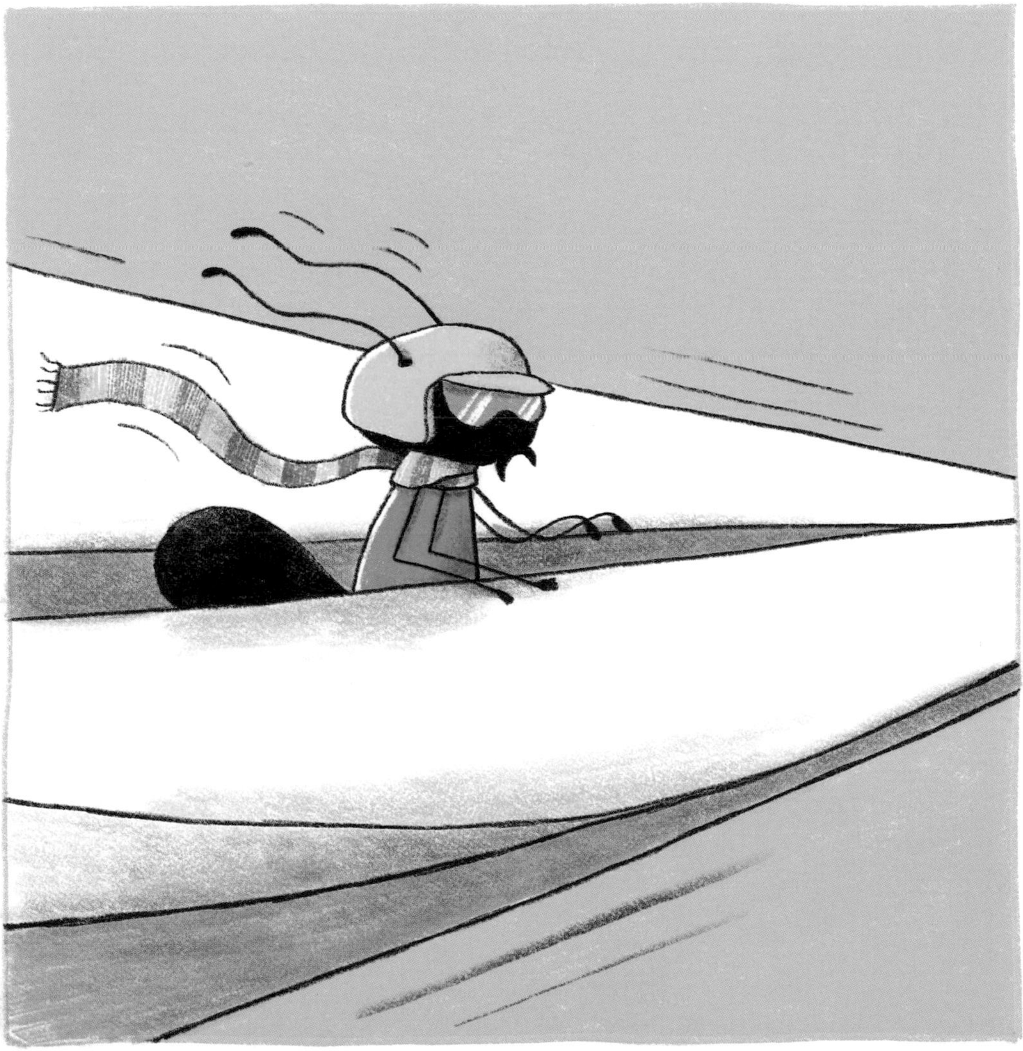

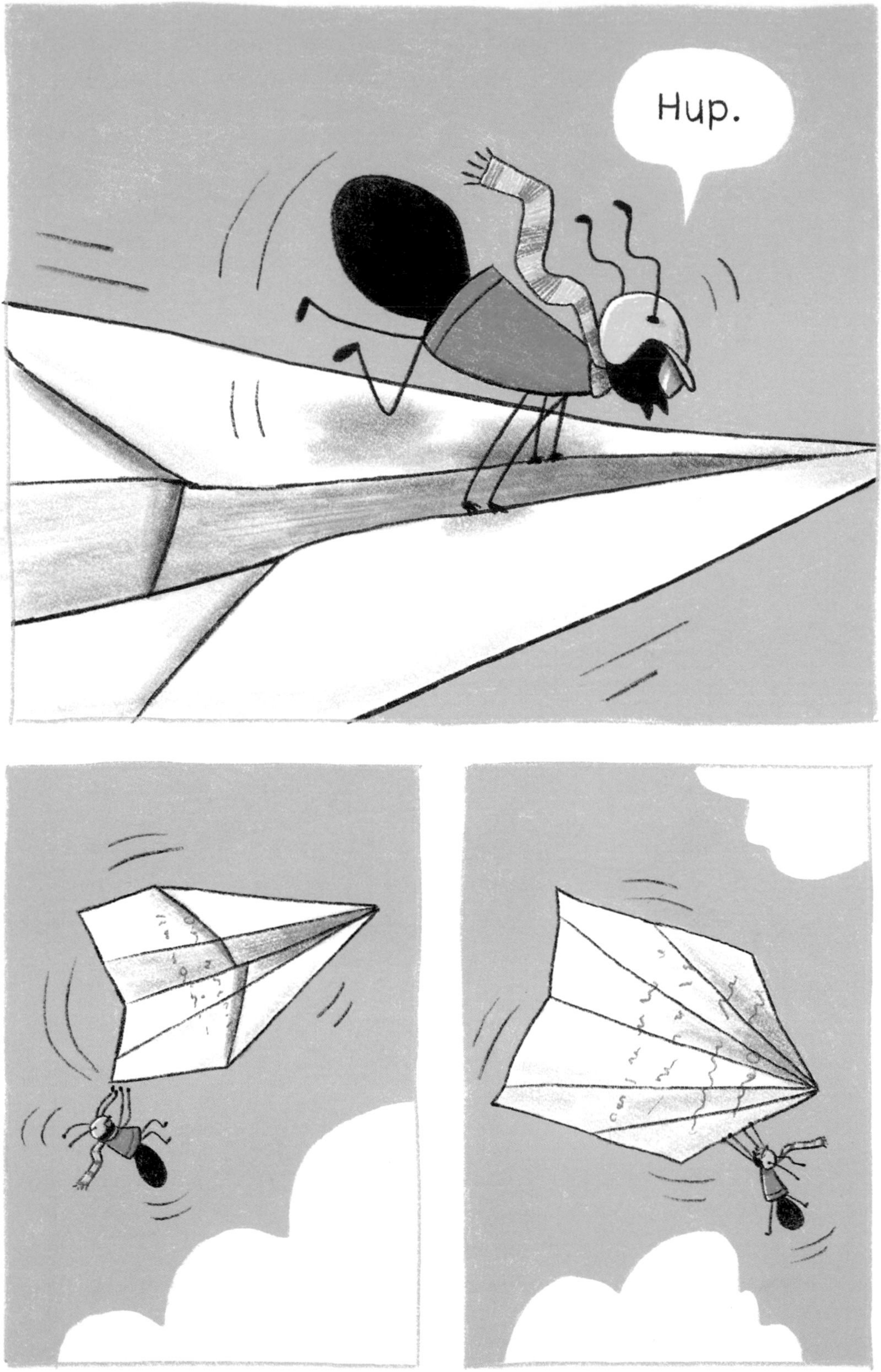
Hup.

LIBRARY NOTICE
LIBRARY NOTICE

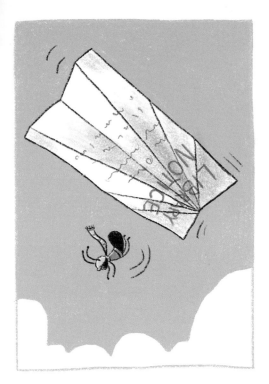

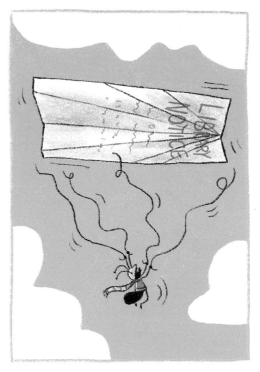

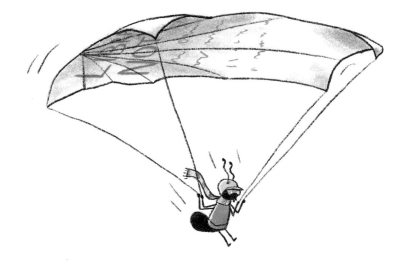

Chapter 1:
Almost Overdue

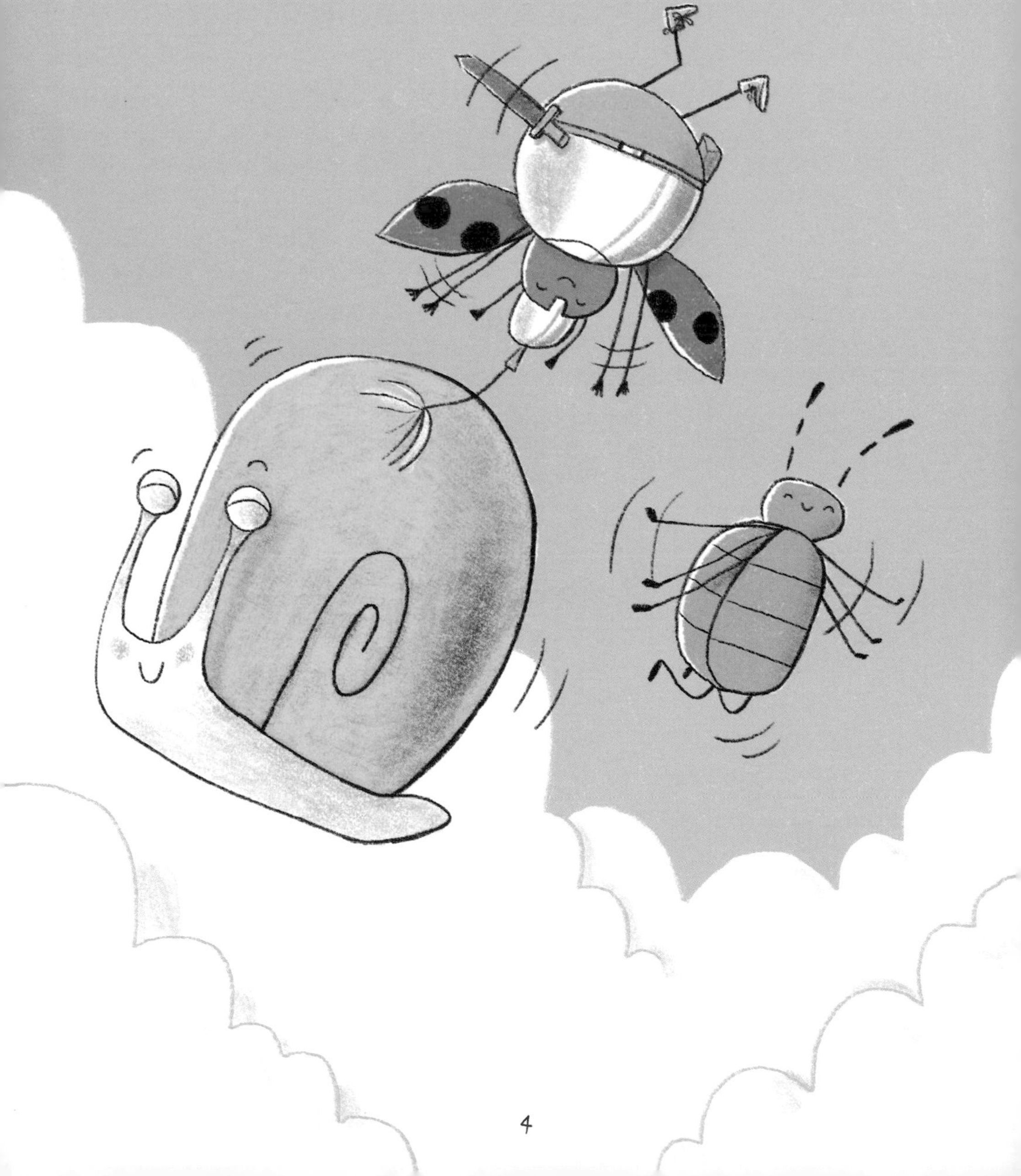

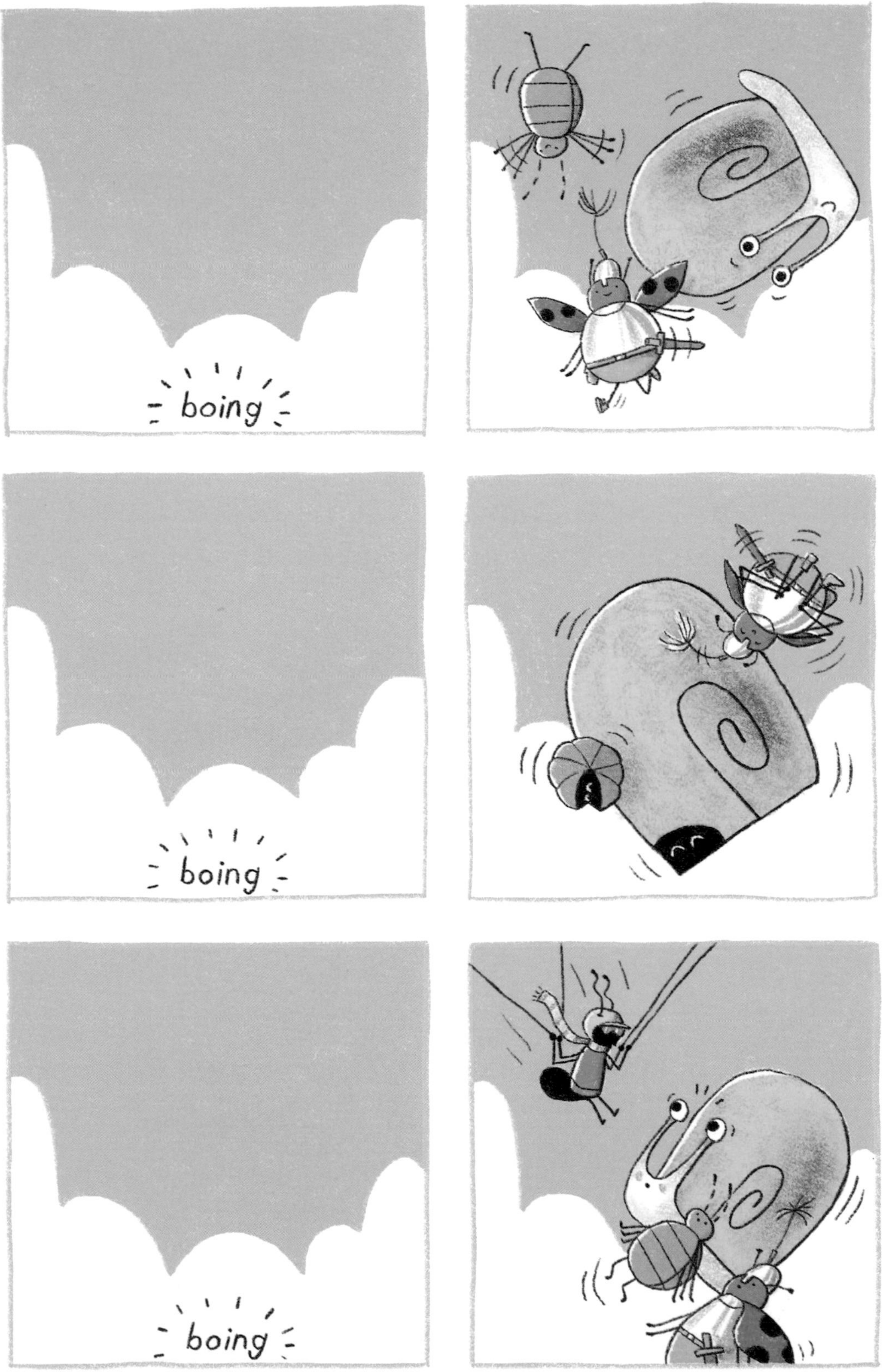
boing
boing
boing

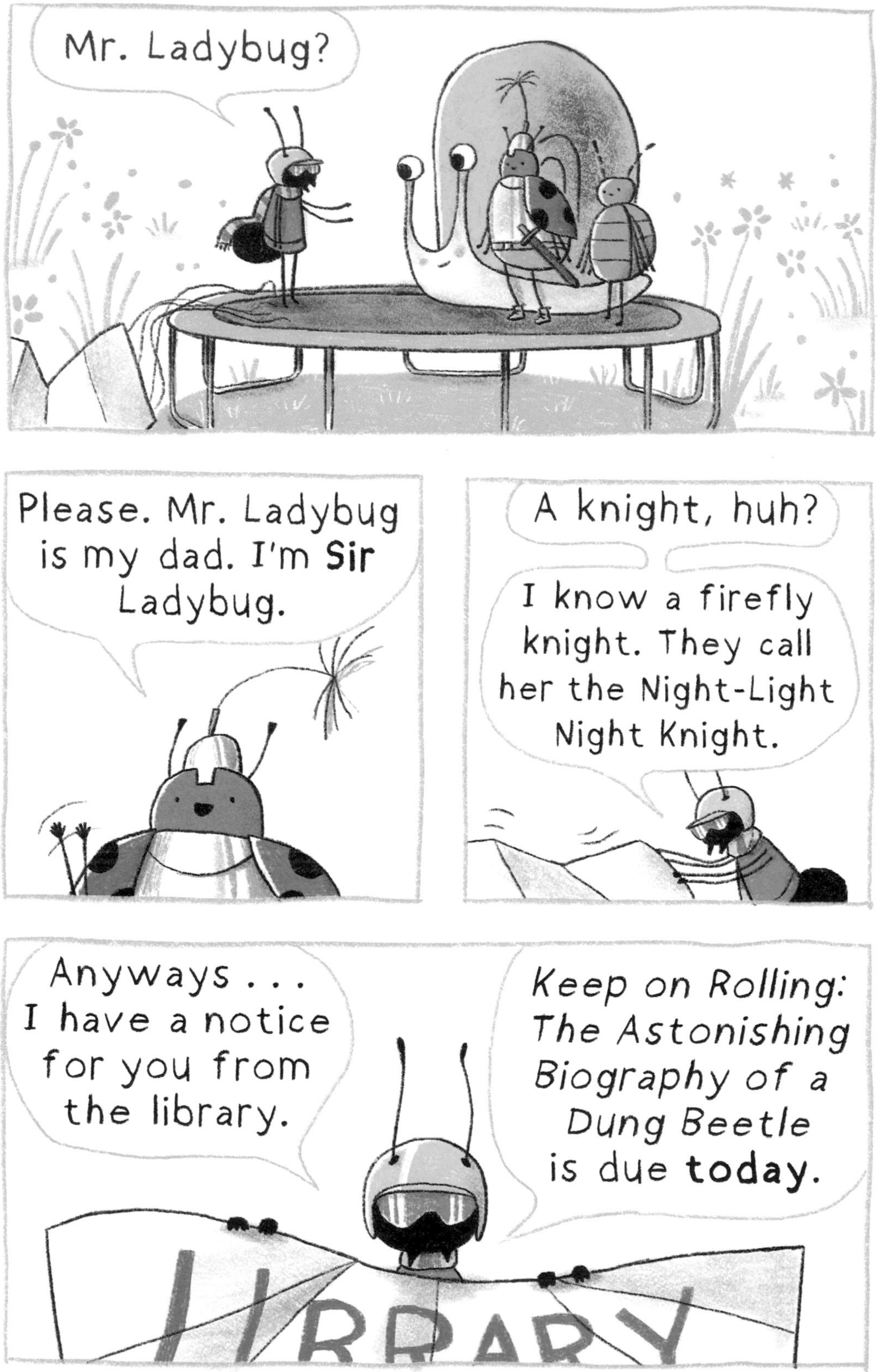
Mr. Ladybug?
Please. Mr. Ladybug is my dad. I'm **Sir** Ladybug.
A knight, huh?
I know a firefly knight. They call her the Night-Light Night Knight.
Anyways . . . I have a notice for you from the library.
Keep on Rolling: The Astonishing Biography of a Dung Beetle is due **today**.
LIBRARY

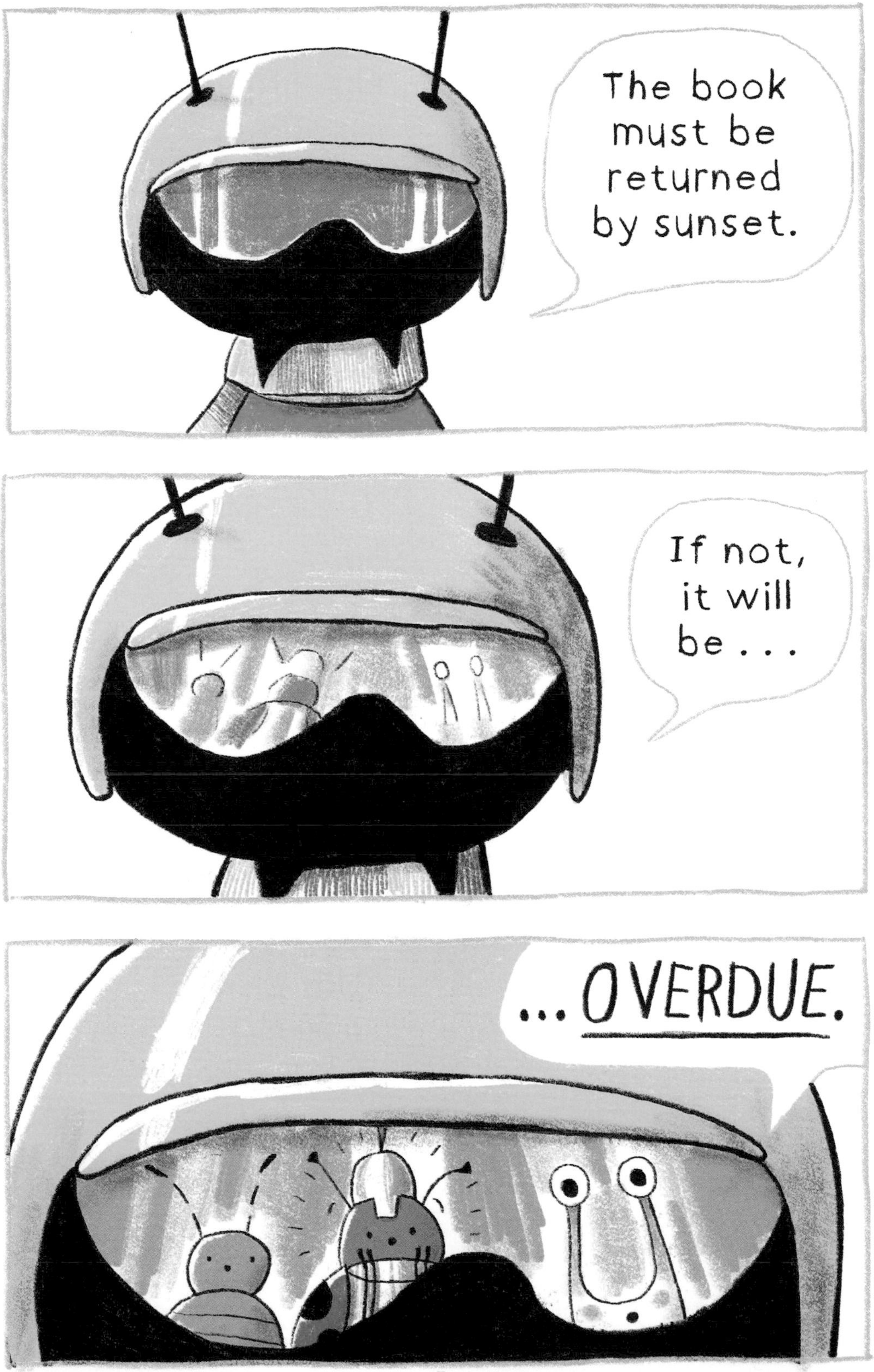
The book must be returned by sunset.
If not, it will be . . .
...OVERDUE.

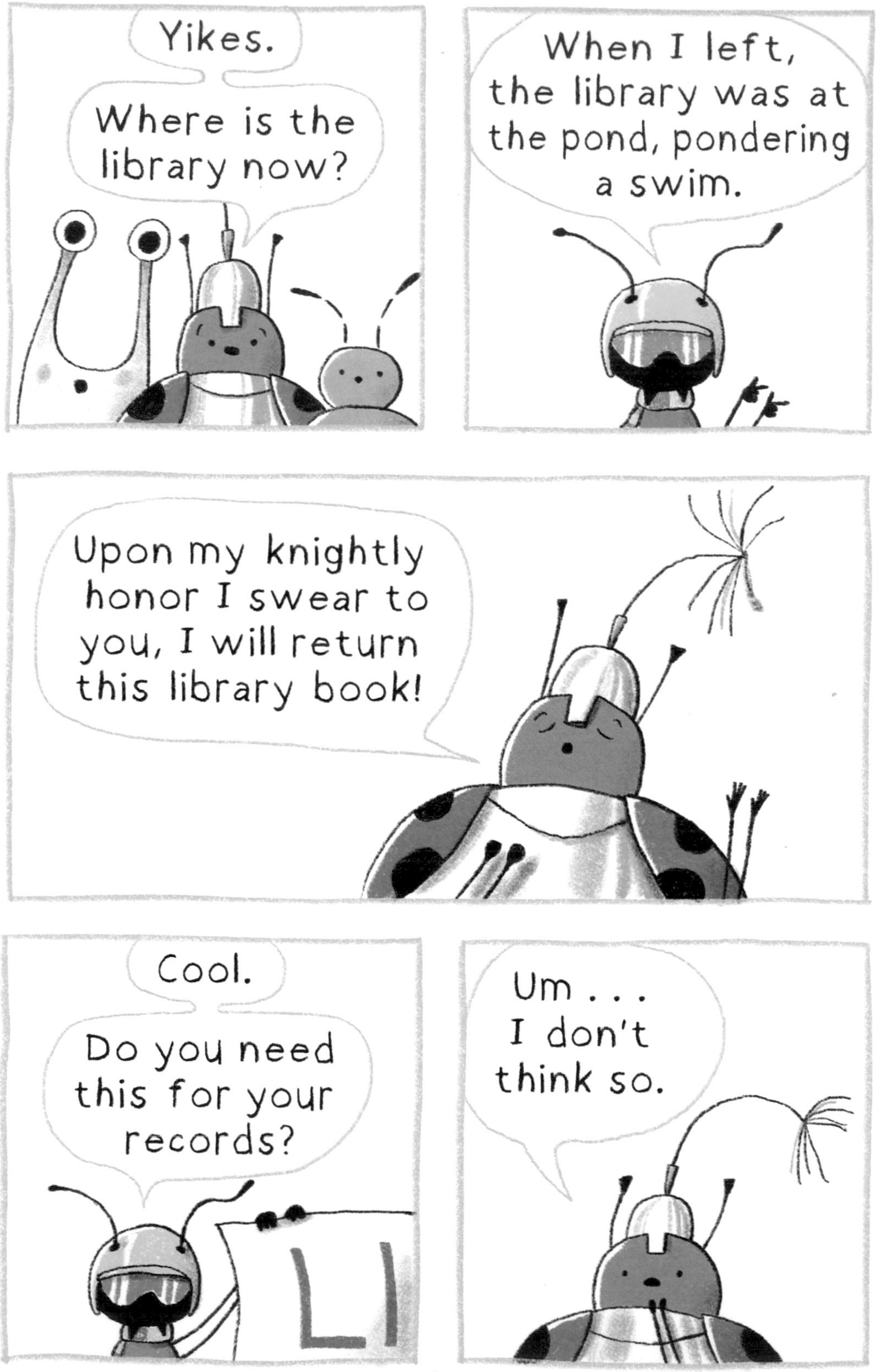
Yikes.
Where is the library now?
When I left, the library was at the pond, pondering a swim.
Upon my knightly honor I swear to you, I will return this library book!
Cool.
Do you need this for your records?
LI
Um . . . I don't think so.

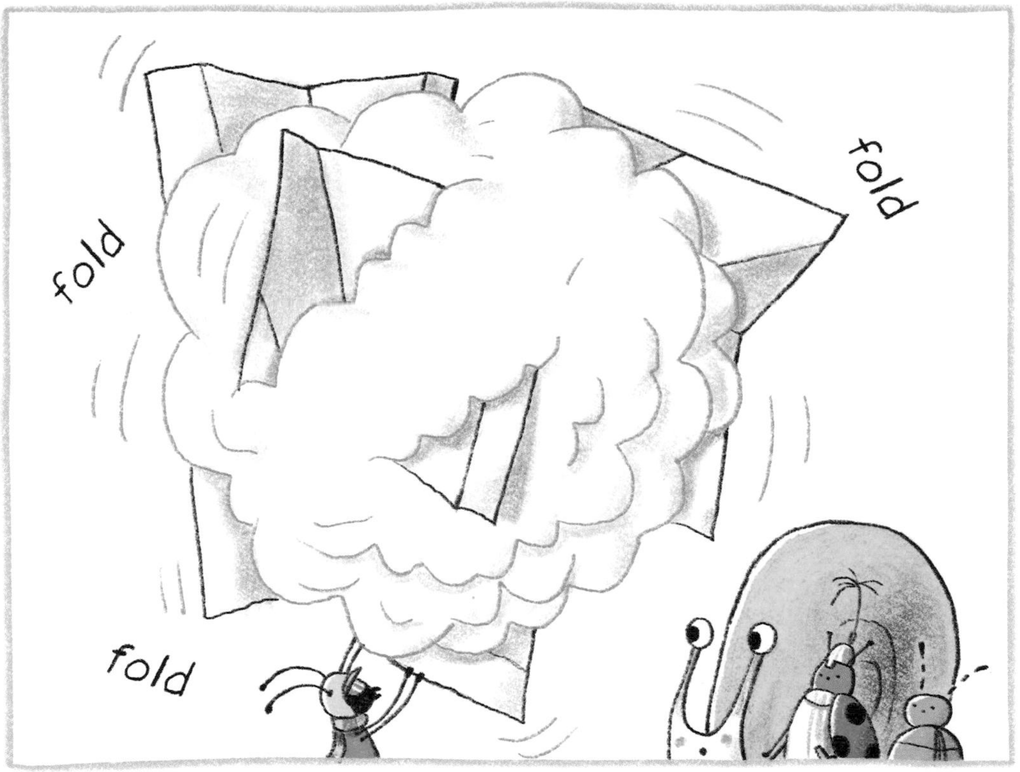
fold
fold
fold

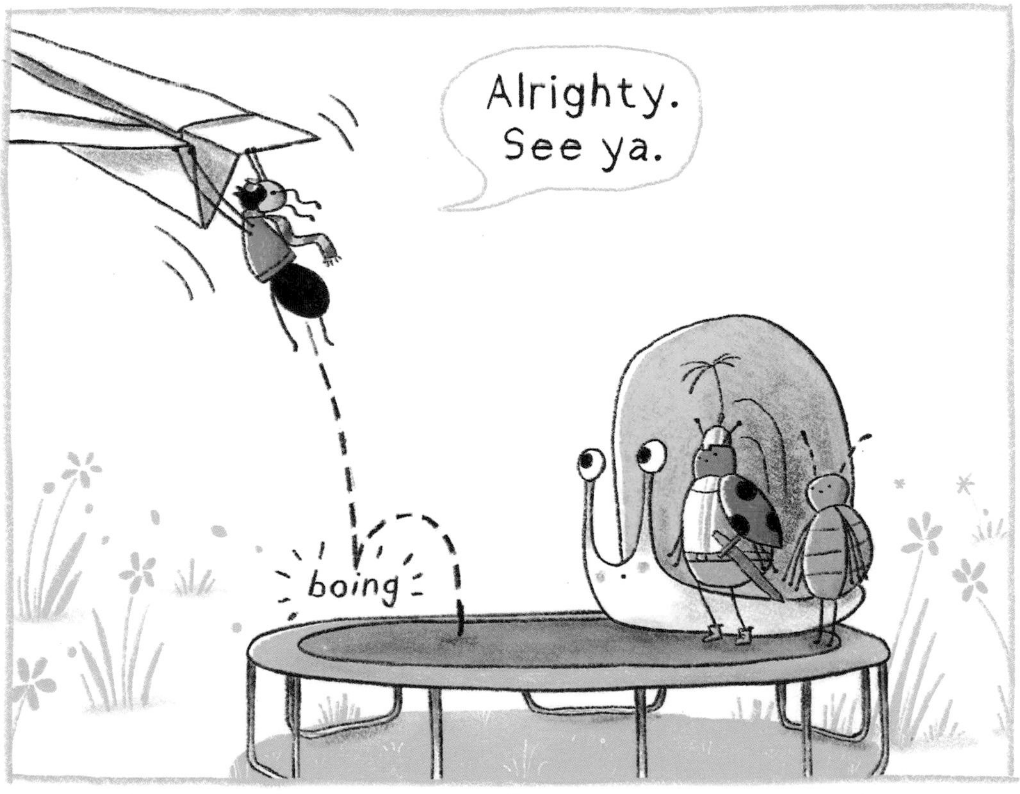
Alrighty. See ya.
boing

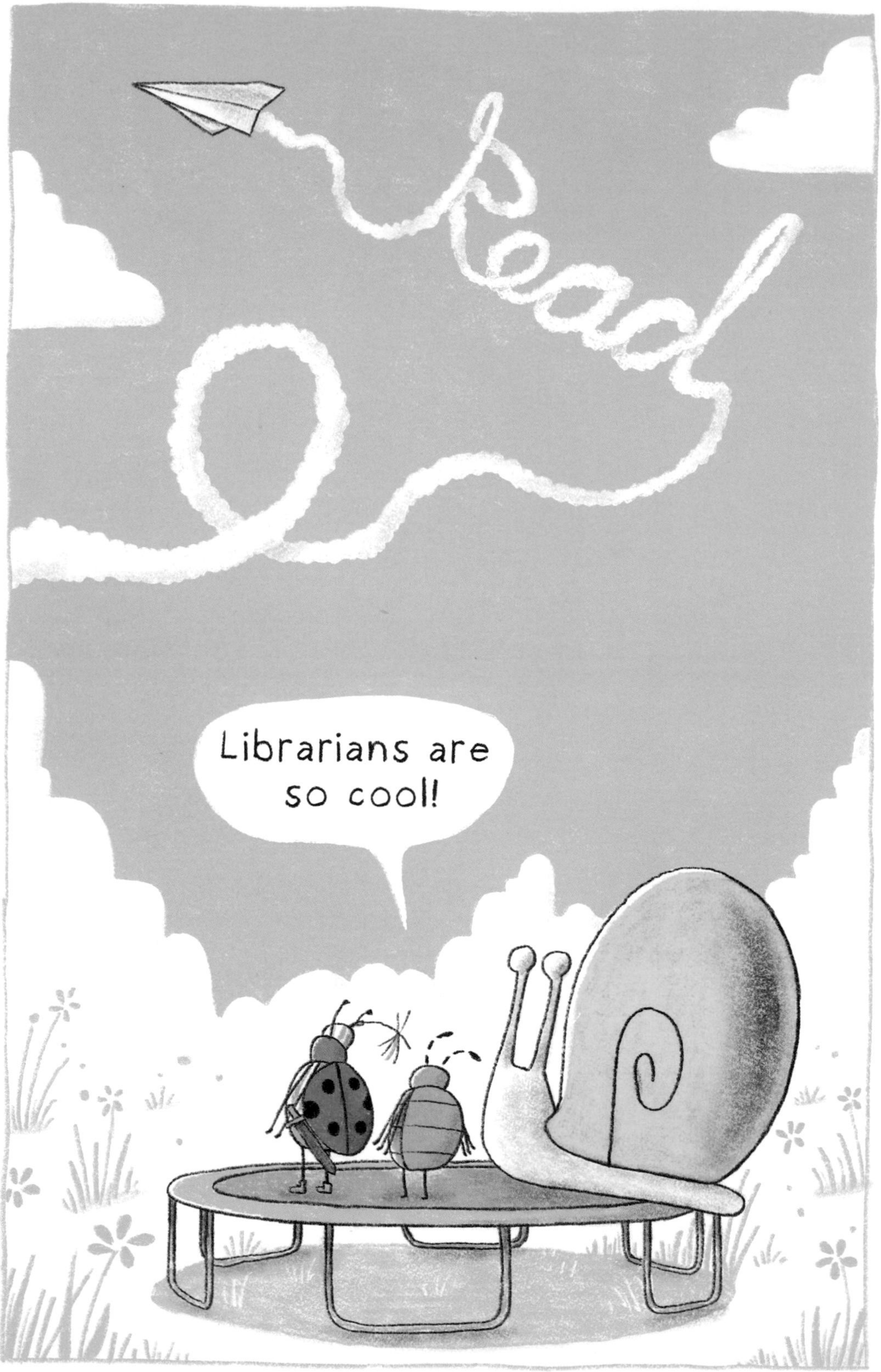
Read
Librarians are so cool!

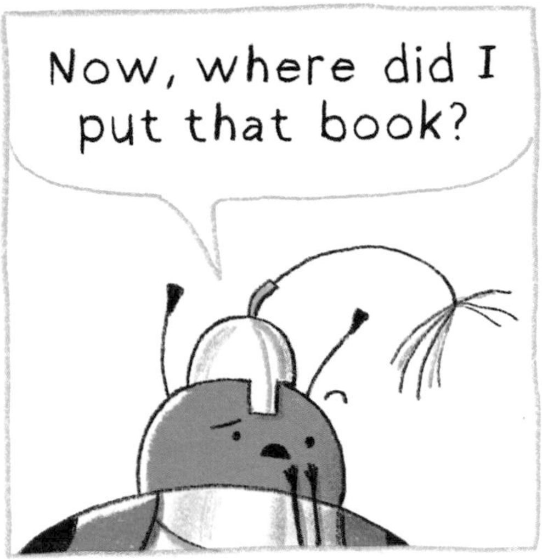
Now, where did I put that book?

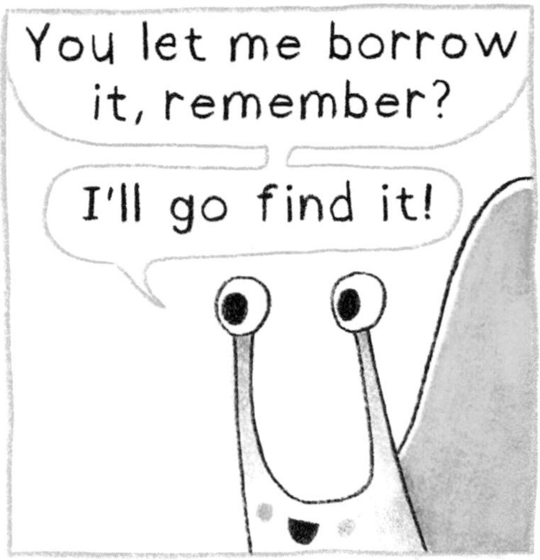
You let me borrow it, remember?
I'll go find it!

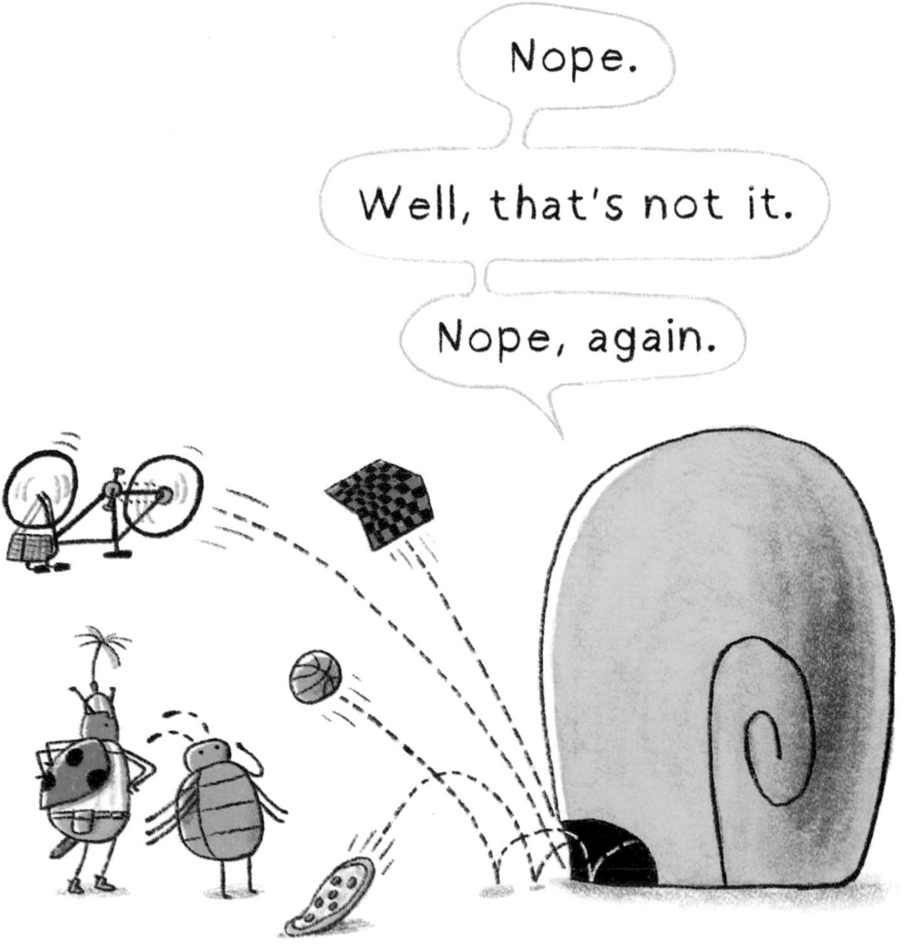
Nope.
Well, that's not it.
Nope, again.

Later . . .

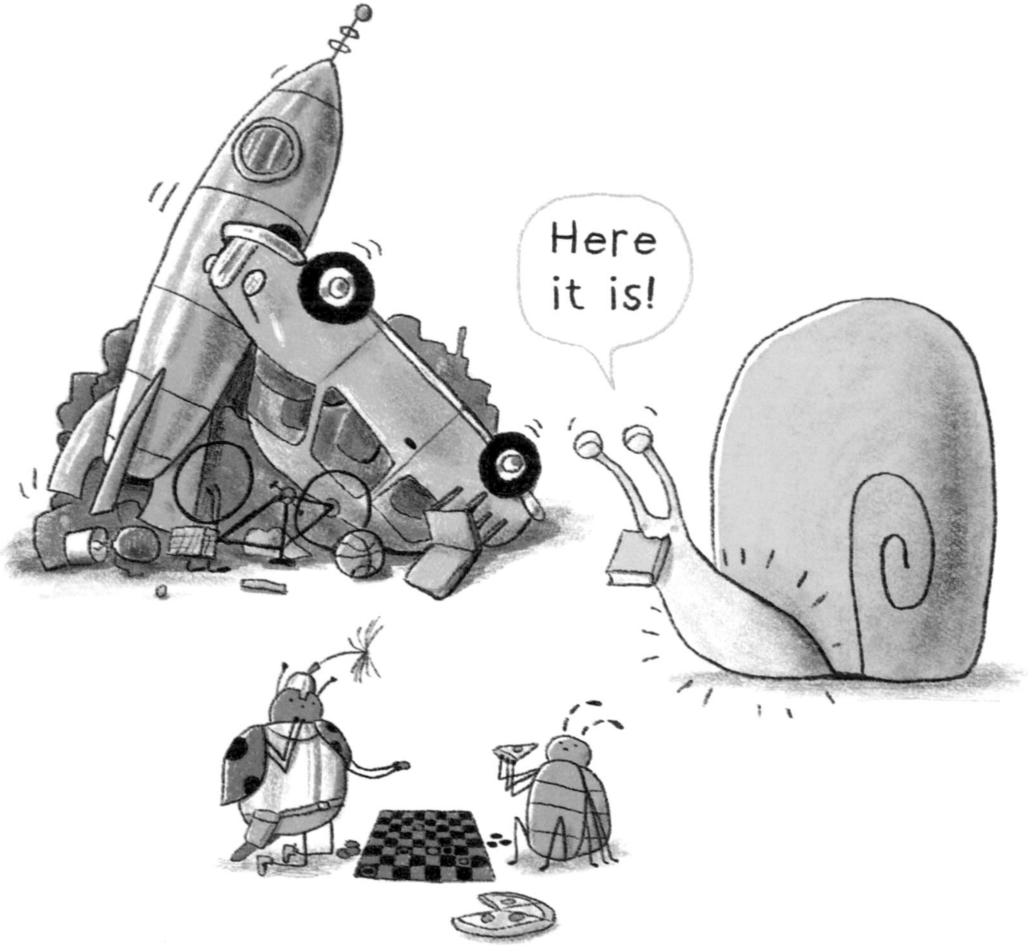
Here it is!

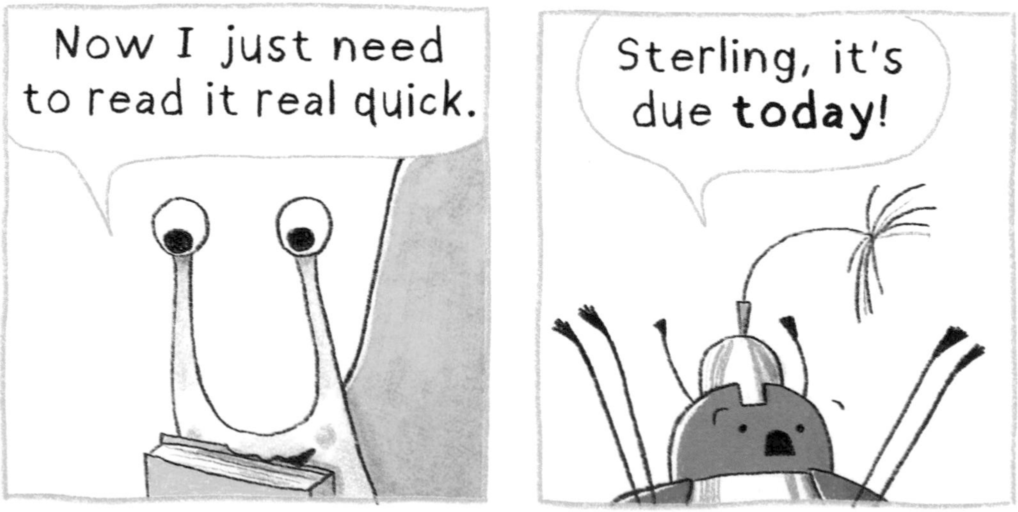
Now I just need to read it real quick.
Sterling, it's due **today**!

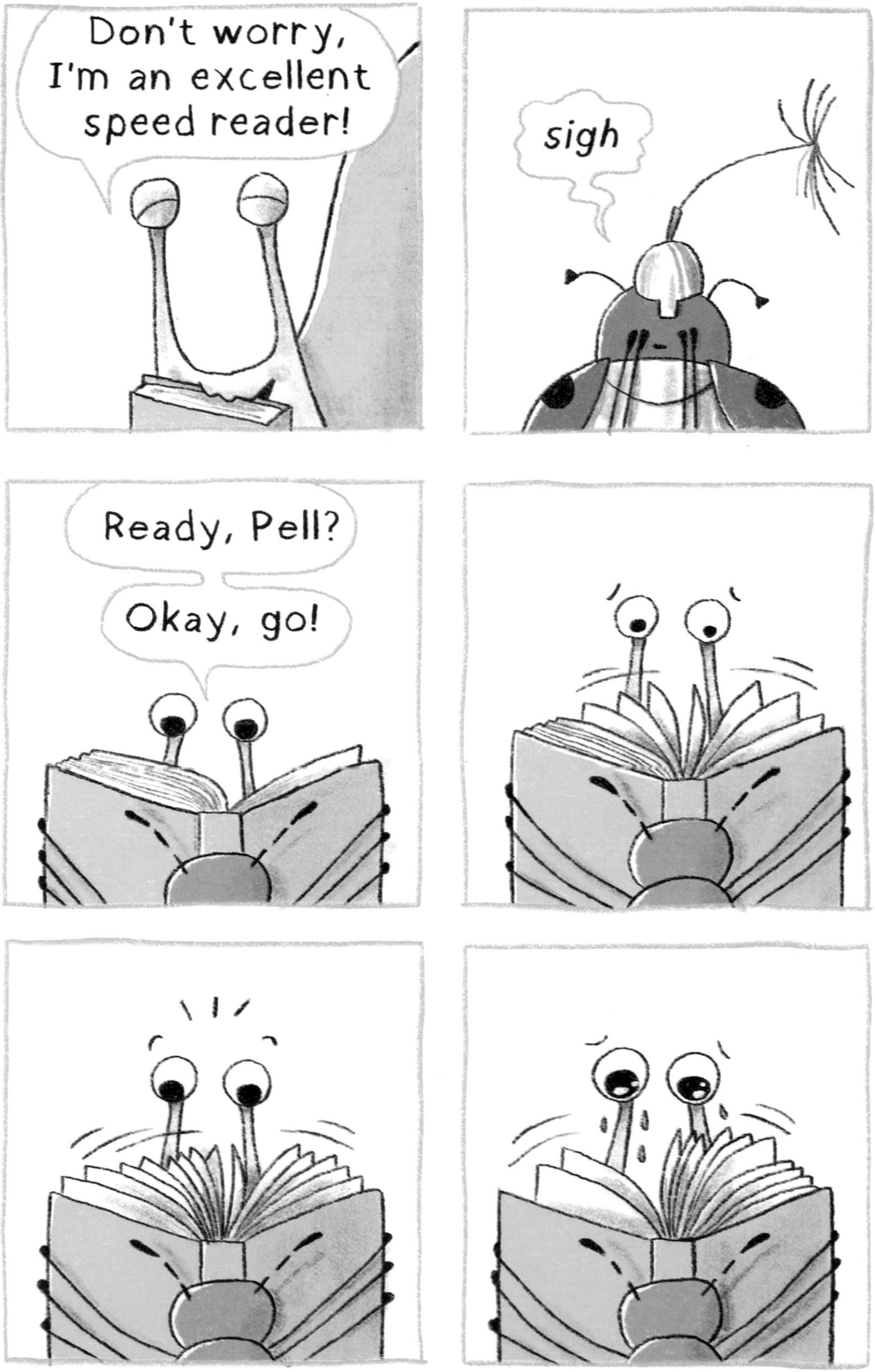
Don't worry, I'm an excellent speed reader!
sigh
Ready, Pell?
Okay, go!

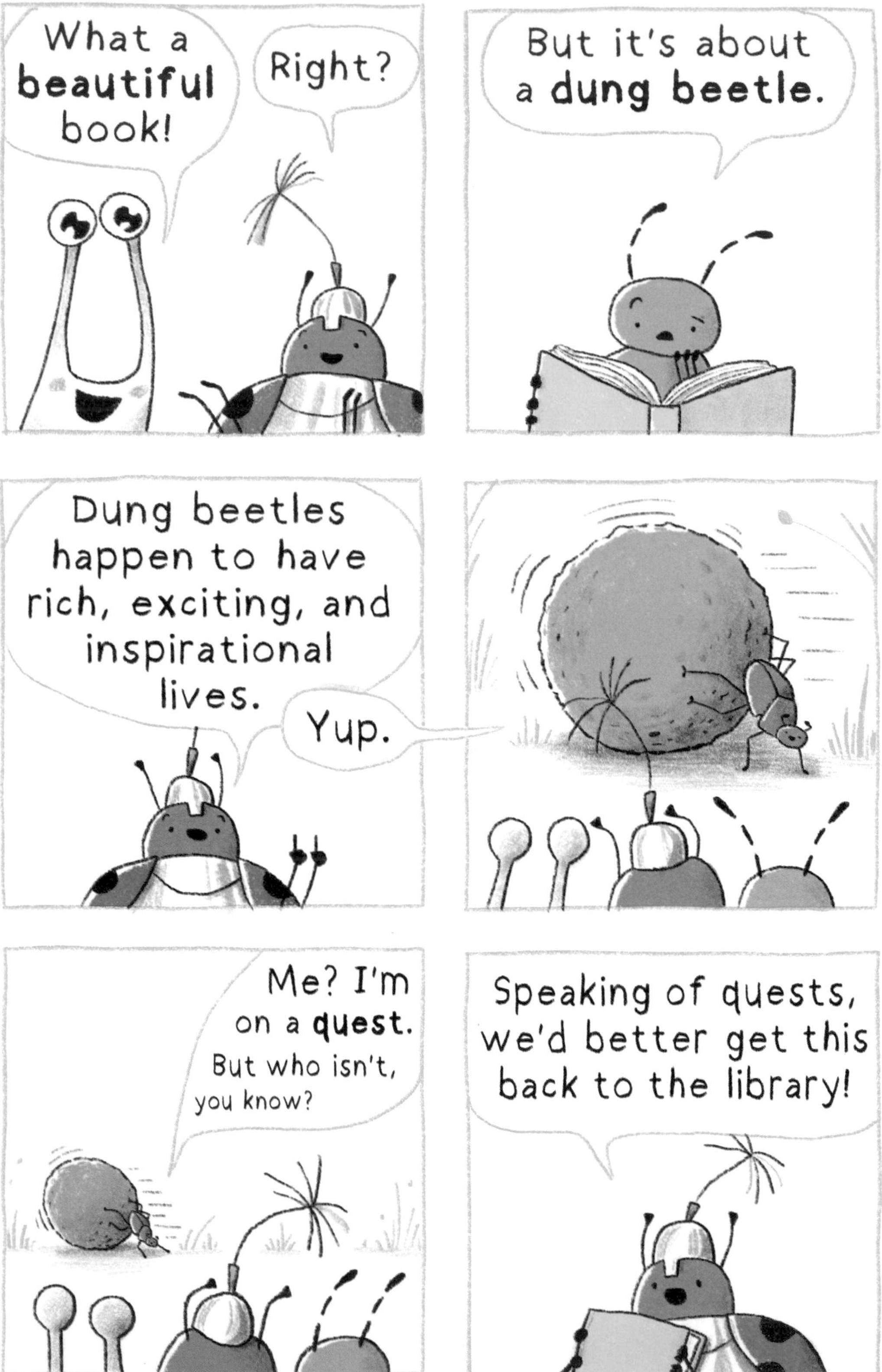
What a **beautiful** book!
Right?
But it's about a **dung beetle.**
Dung beetles happen to have rich, exciting, and inspirational lives.
Yup.
Me? I'm on a **quest.**
But who isn't, you know?
Speaking of quests, we'd better get this back to the library!

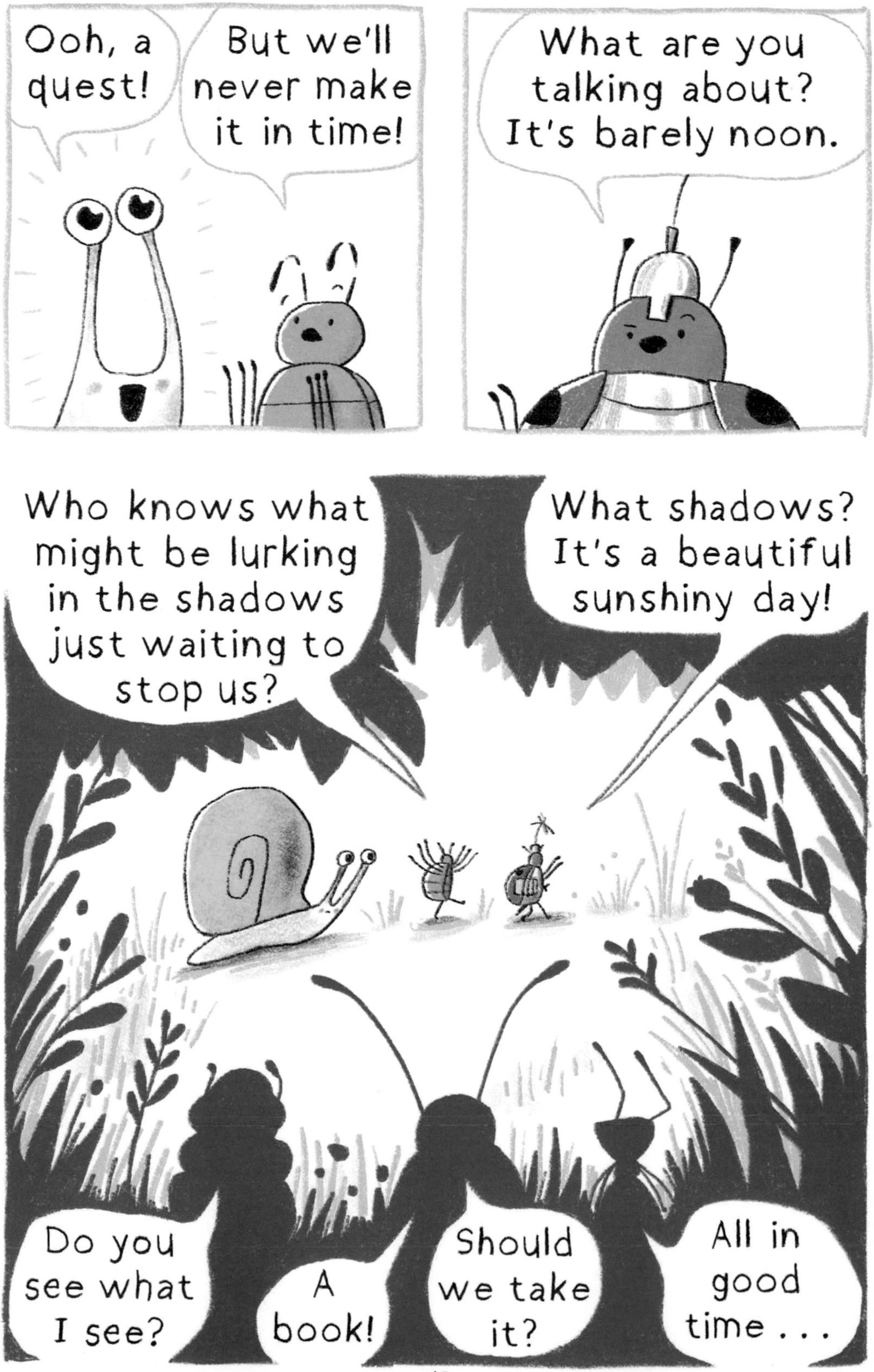
Ooh, a quest!
But we'll never make it in time!
What are you talking about? It's barely noon.
Who knows what might be lurking in the shadows just waiting to stop us?
What shadows? It's a beautiful sunshiny day!
Do you see what I see?
A book!
Should we take it?
All in good time . . .

A short excerpt from
**Keep on Rolling:
The Astonishing
Biography of a
Dung Beetle**

Chapter 1
The Metamorphosis

One morning Gregor woke to discover that he was a dung beetle. Which was good, because that was exactly how he went to bed.

But Gregor had a friend who once went to bed as a caterpillar and woke up as a butterfly, so you never did know . . .

Chapter 2: HELP!

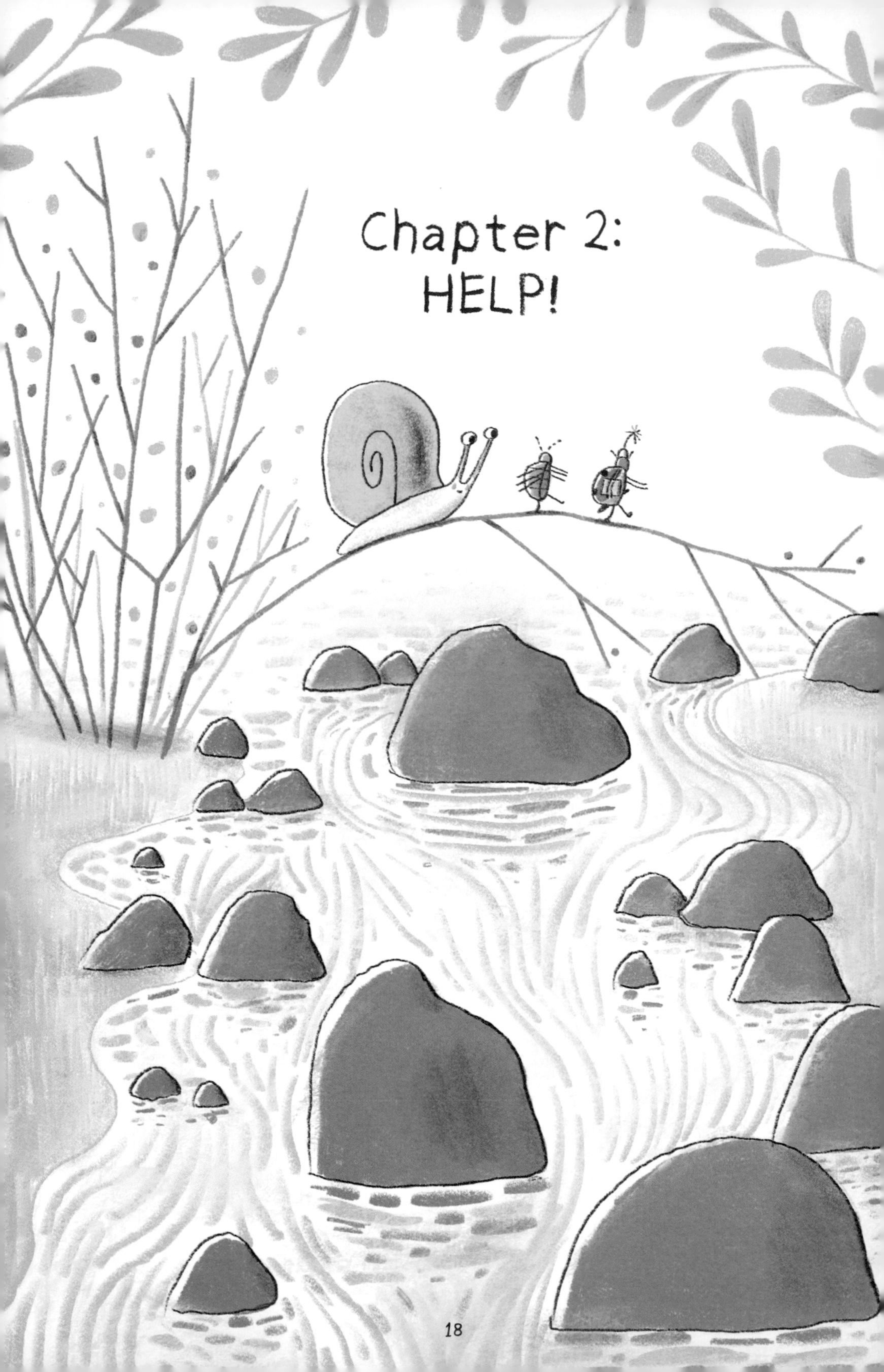

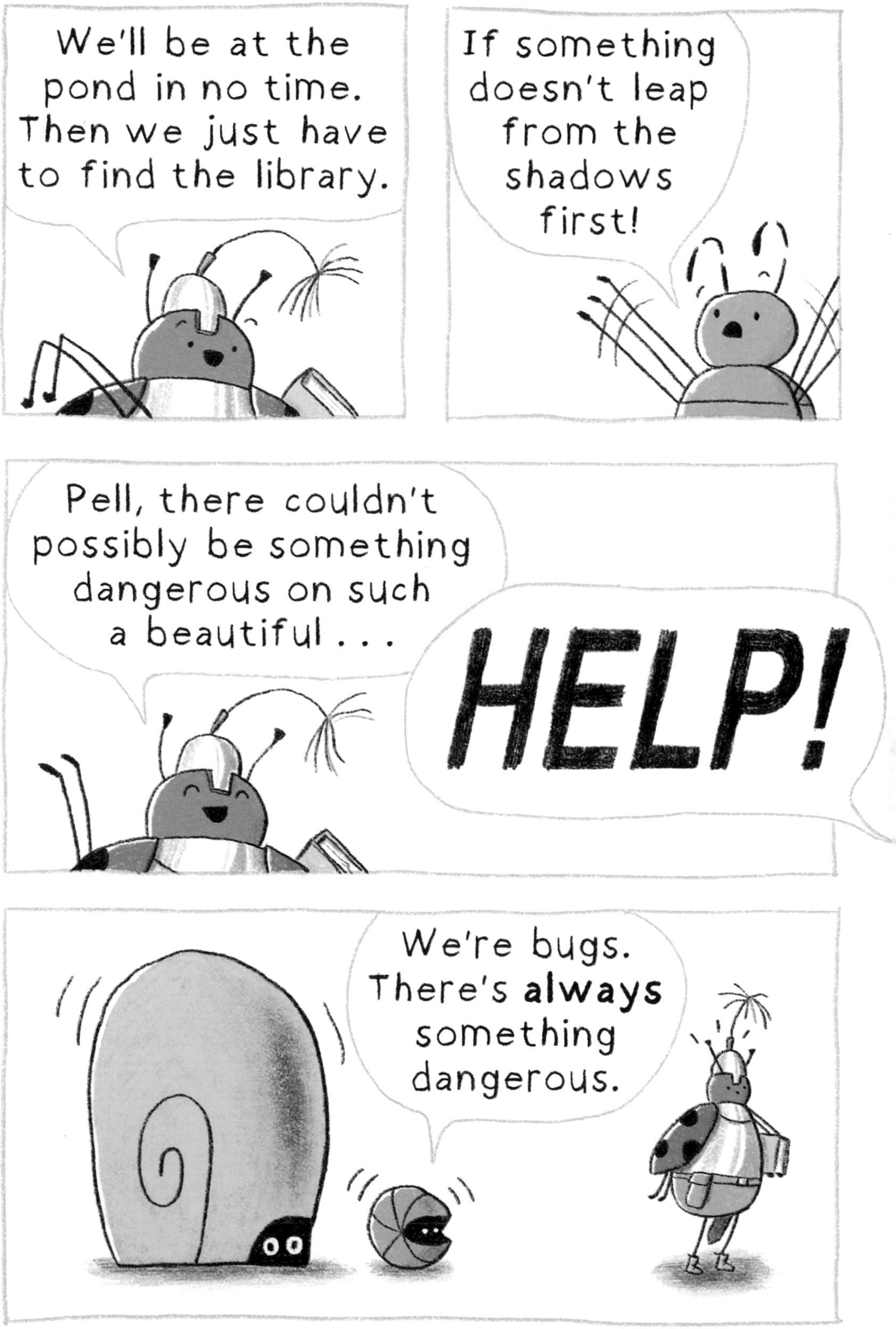
We'll be at the pond in no time. Then we just have to find the library.
If something doesn't leap from the shadows first!
Pell, there couldn't possibly be something dangerous on such a beautiful . . .
HELP!
We're bugs. There's **always** something dangerous.

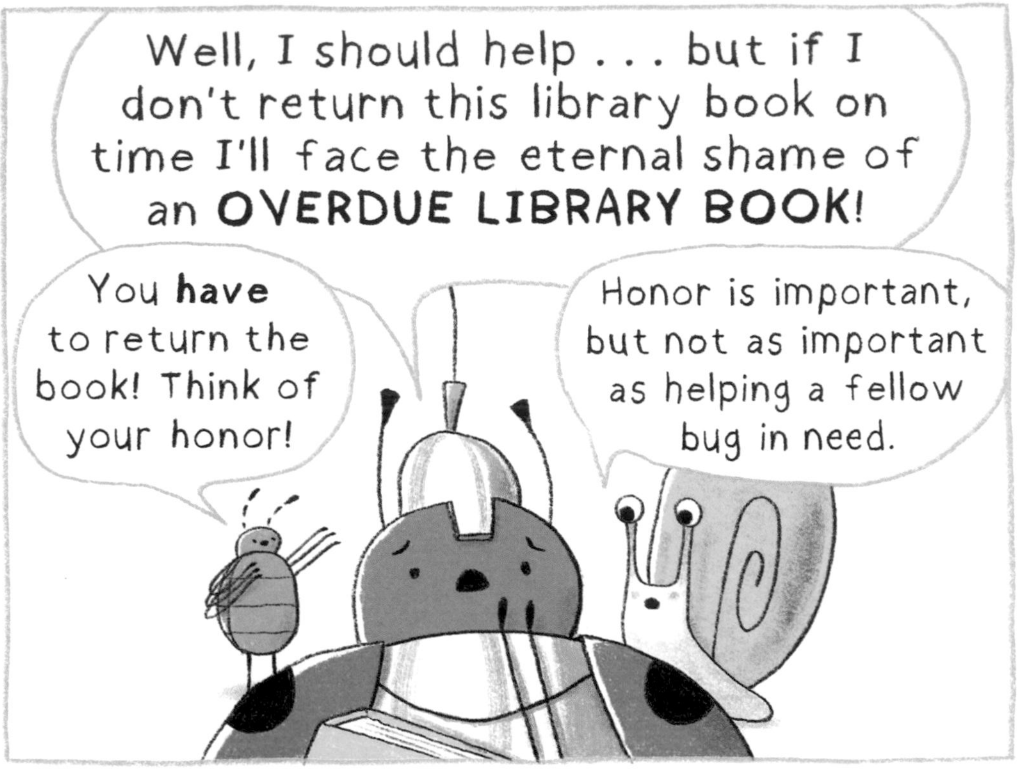
Well, I should help . . . but if I don't return this library book on time I'll face the eternal shame of an **OVERDUE LIBRARY BOOK**!
You **have** to return the book! Think of your honor!
Honor is important, but not as important as helping a fellow bug in need.

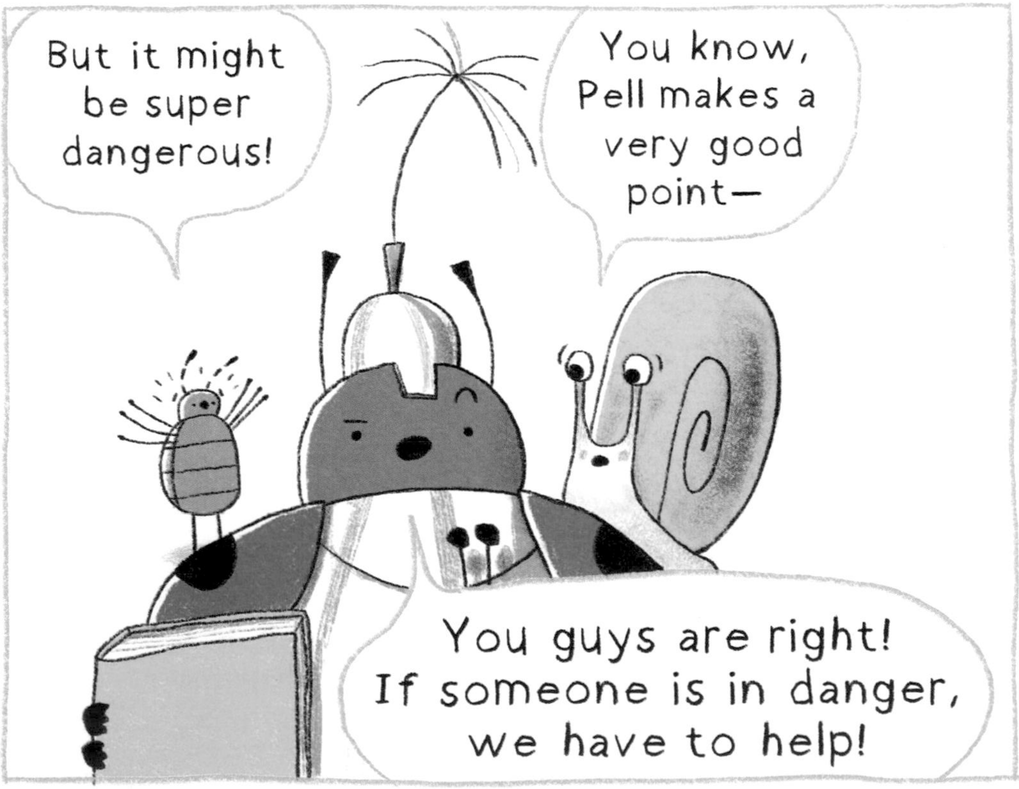
But it might be super dangerous!
You know, Pell makes a very good point—
You guys are right! If someone is in danger, we have to help!

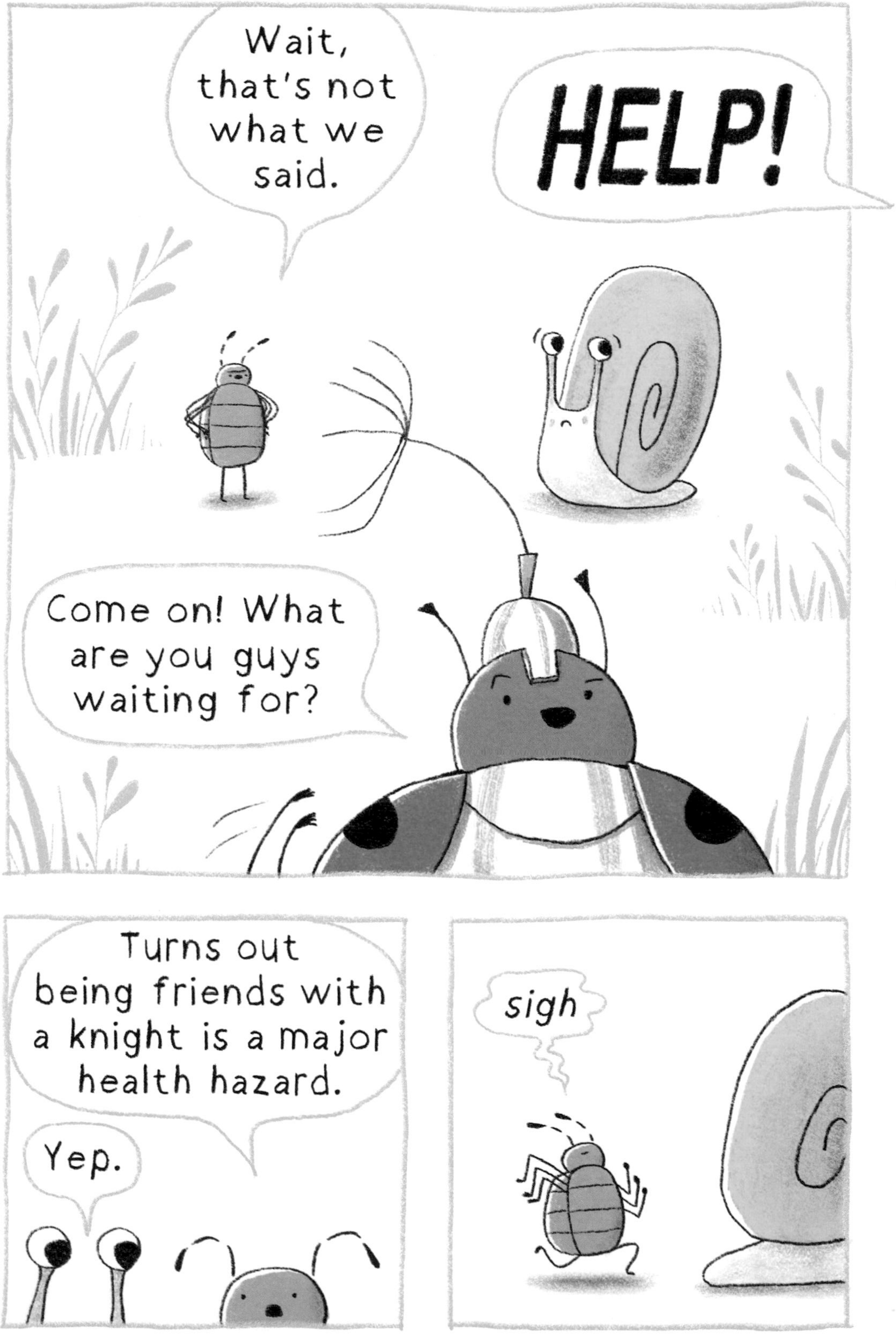
Wait, that's not what we said.
HELP!
Come on! What are you guys waiting for?
Turns out being friends with a knight is a major health hazard.
Yep.
sigh

HEL—

Oh, hi! Sorry about all the yelling. It's just, I've been trying to figure out what to do about this pine cone and I'm stumped.

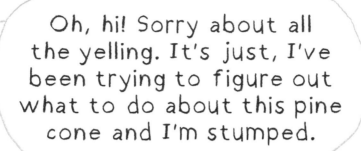

What about going around it?

Have **you** ever tried steering one of these things? It's harder than it looks.

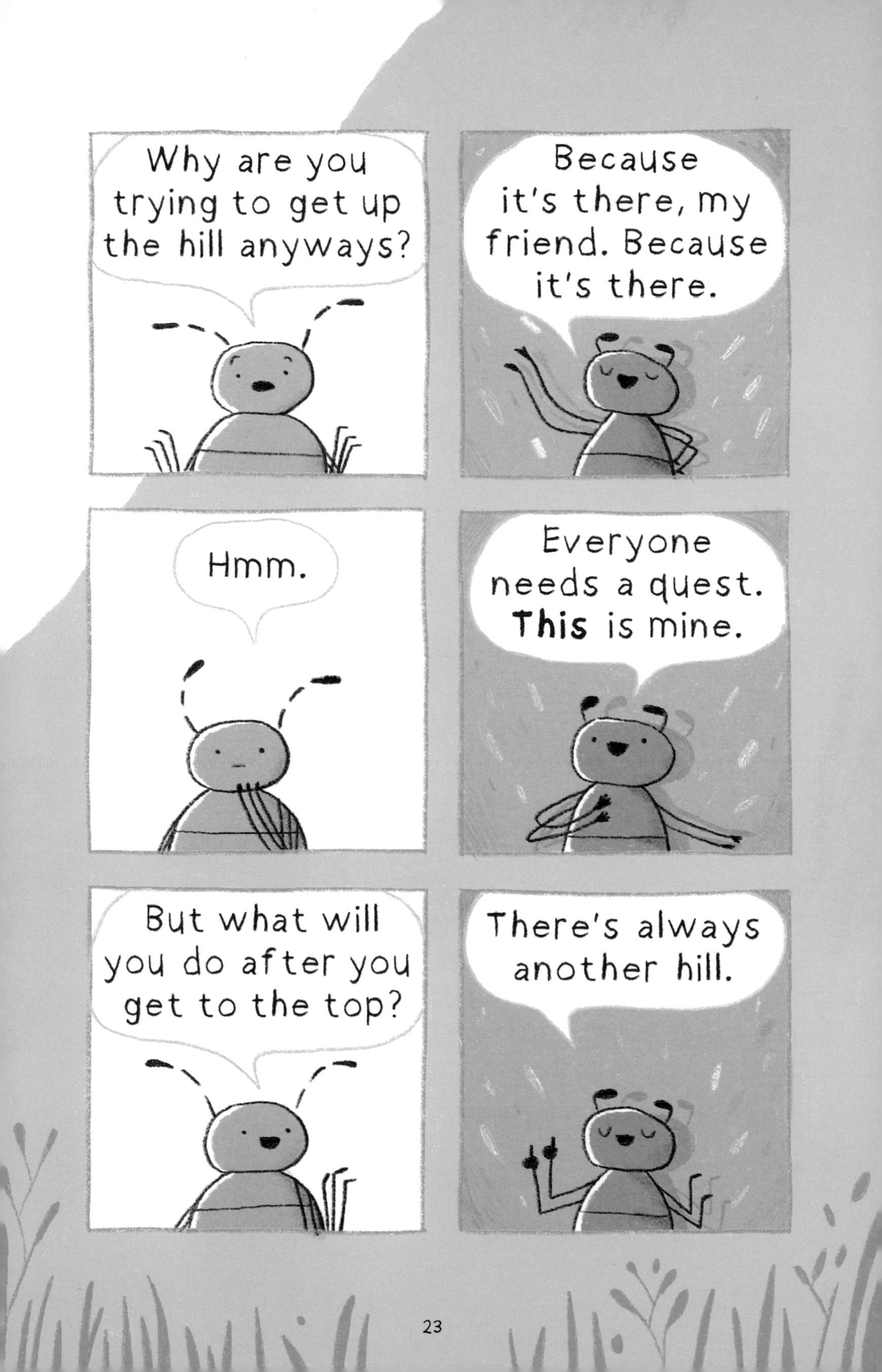
Why are you trying to get up the hill anyways?
Because it's there, my friend. Because it's there.
Hmm.
Everyone needs a quest. **This** is mine.
But what will you do after you get to the top?
There's always another hill.

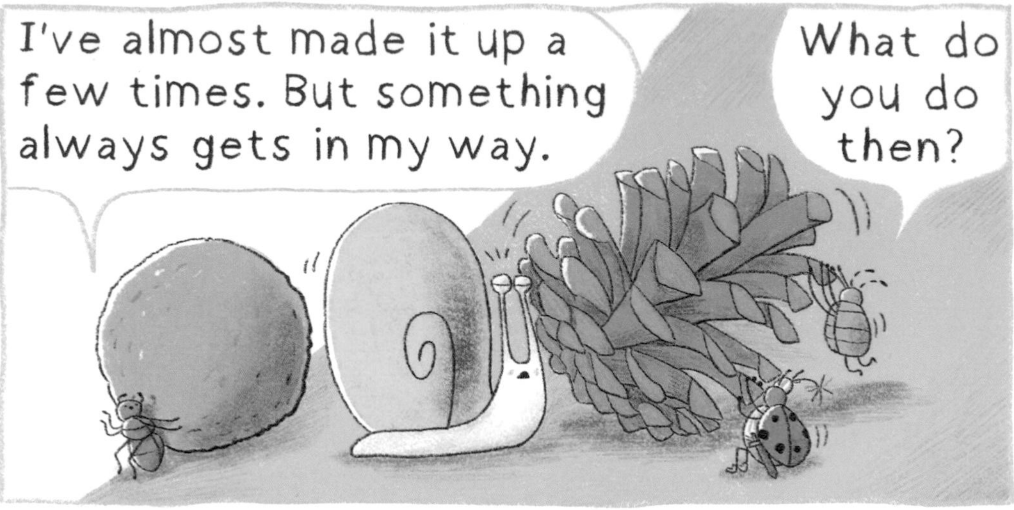
I've almost made it up a few times. But something always gets in my way.
What do you do then?

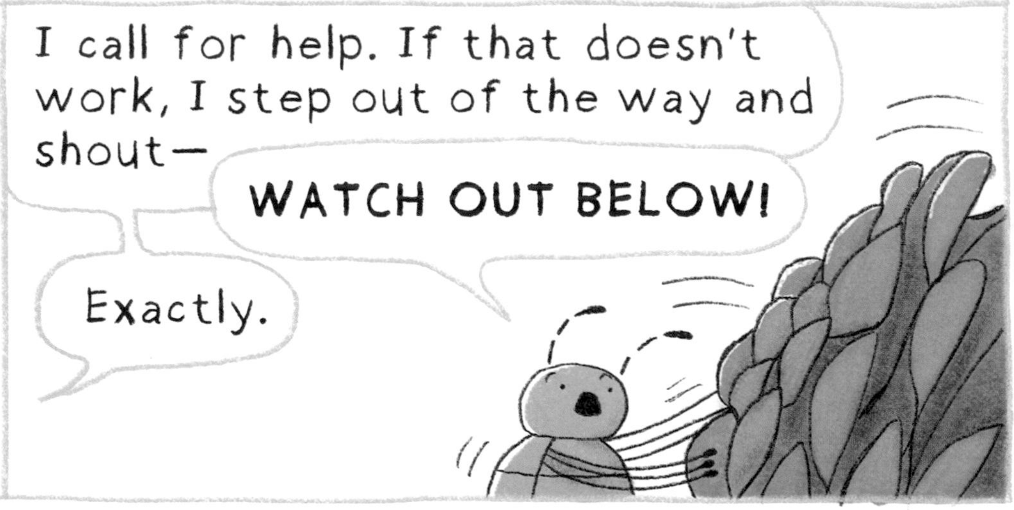
I call for help. If that doesn't work, I step out of the way and shout—
WATCH OUT BELOW!
Exactly.

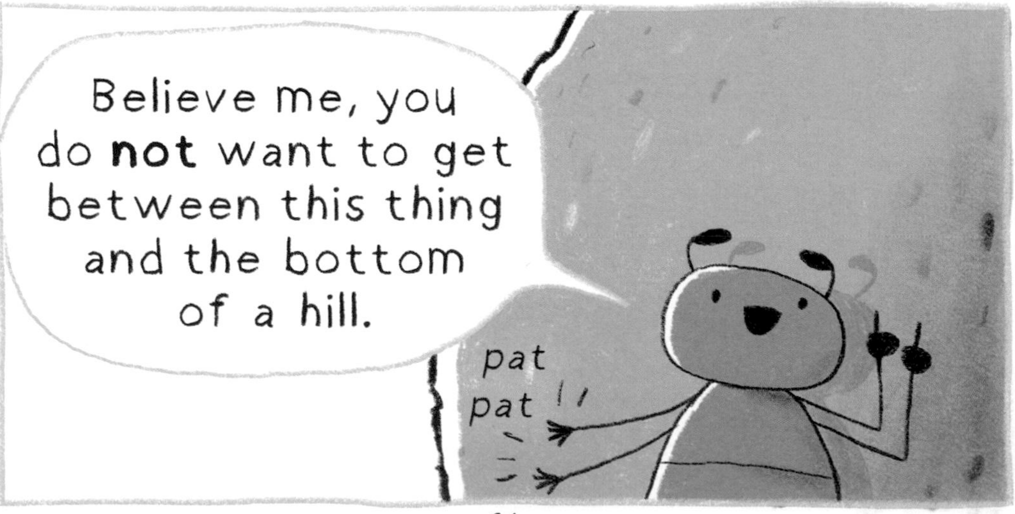
Believe me, you do **not** want to get between this thing and the bottom of a hill.
pat
pat

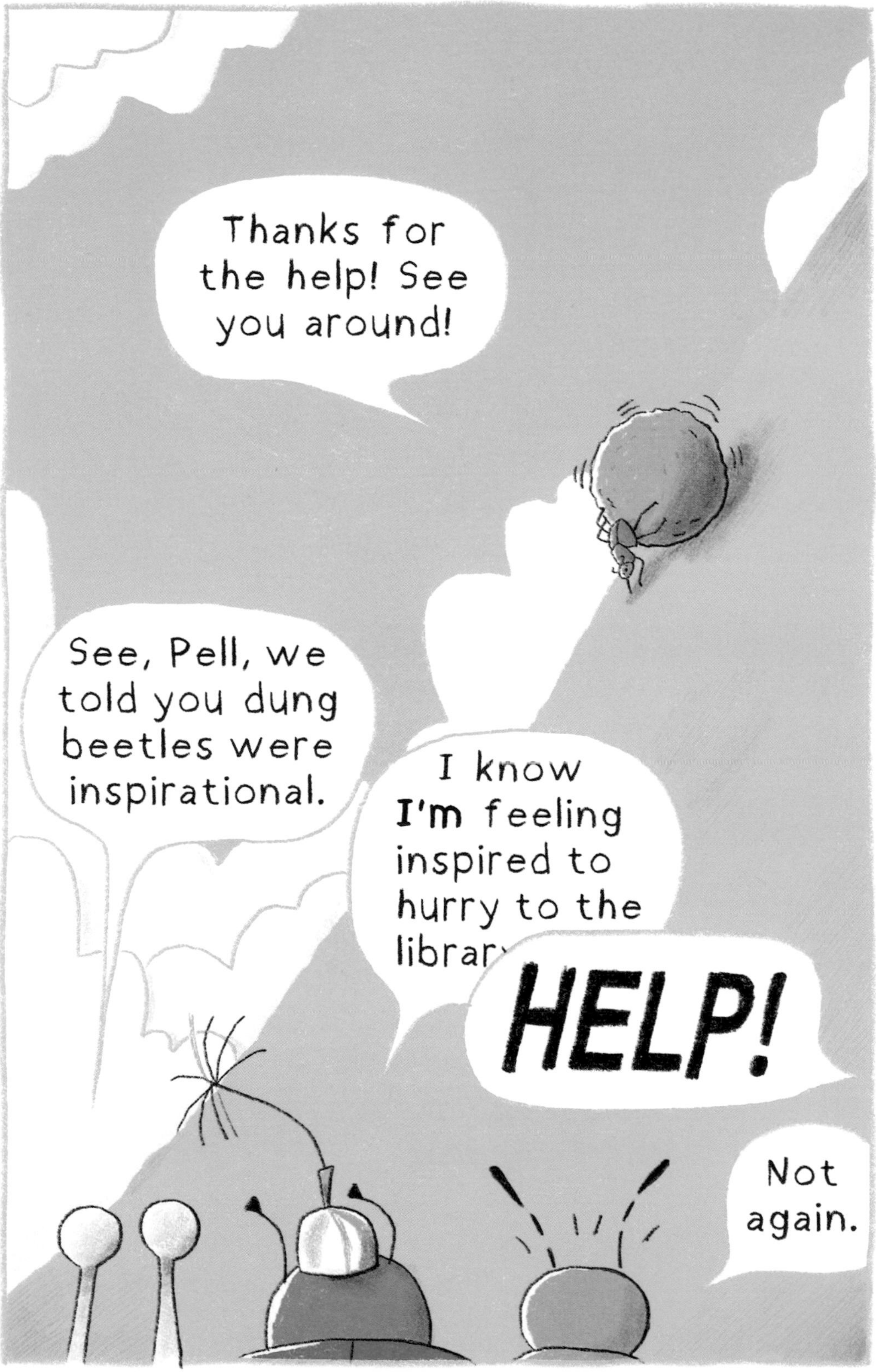
Thanks for the help! See you around!
See, Pell, we told you dung beetles were inspirational.
I know **I'm** feeling inspired to hurry to the librar
HELP!
Not again.

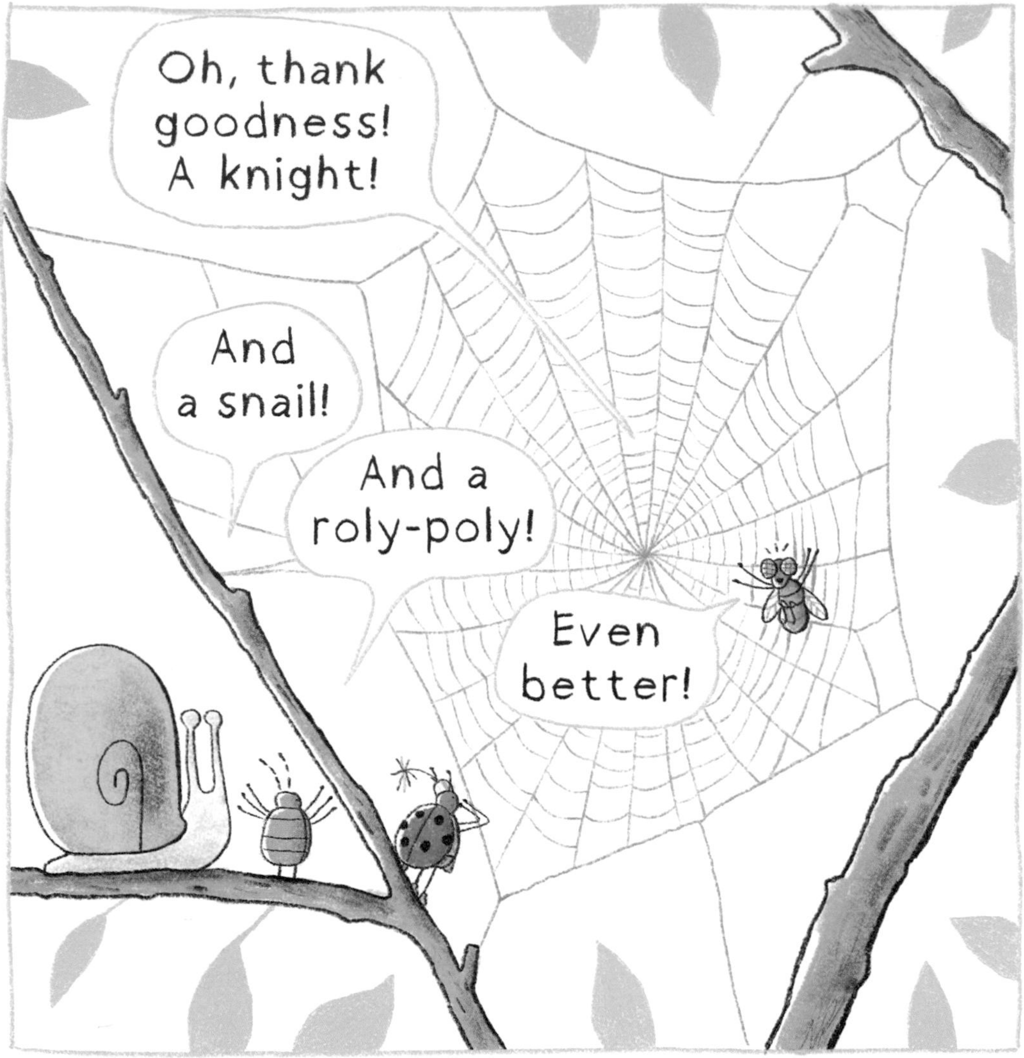
Oh, thank goodness! A knight!
And a snail!
And a roly-poly!
Even better!

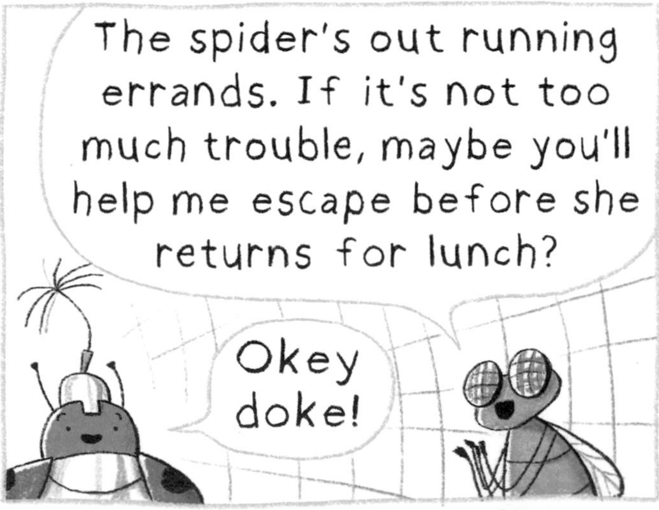
The spider's out running errands. If it's not too much trouble, maybe you'll help me escape before she returns for lunch?
Okey doke!

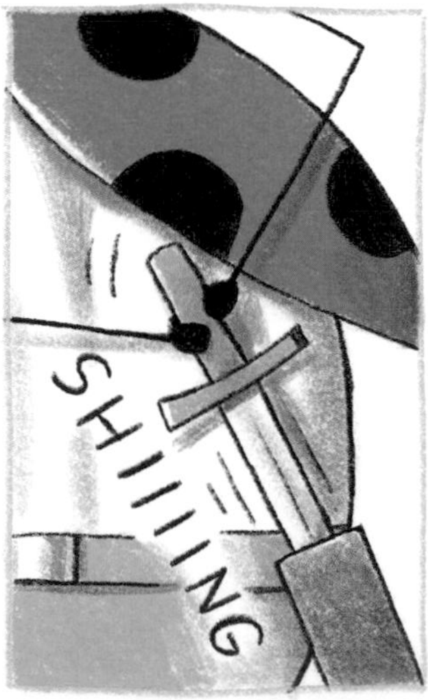
SHIIIING

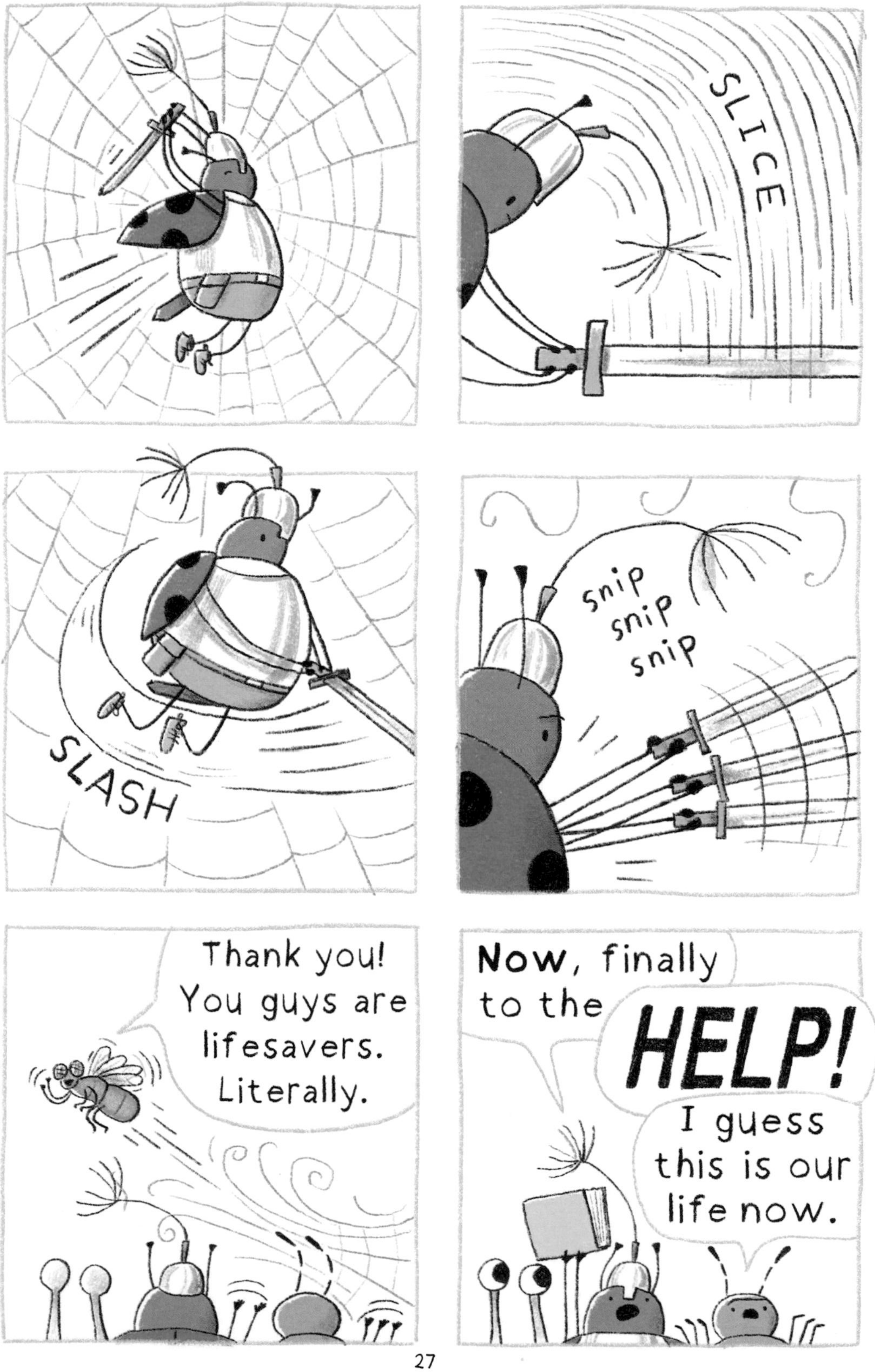
SLICE
SLASH
snip snip snip
Thank you! You guys are lifesavers. Literally.
Now, finally to the HELP!
I guess this is our life now.

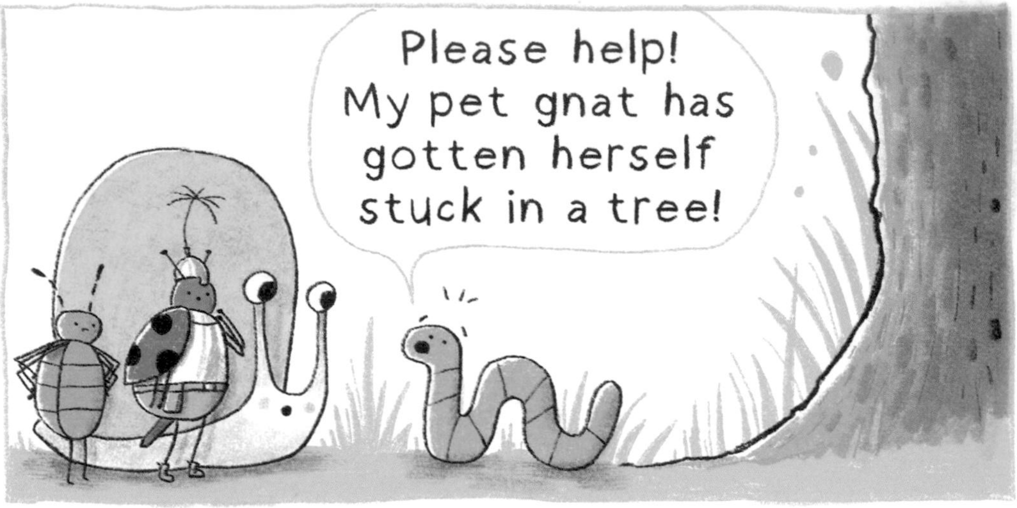
Please help! My pet gnat has gotten herself stuck in a tree!

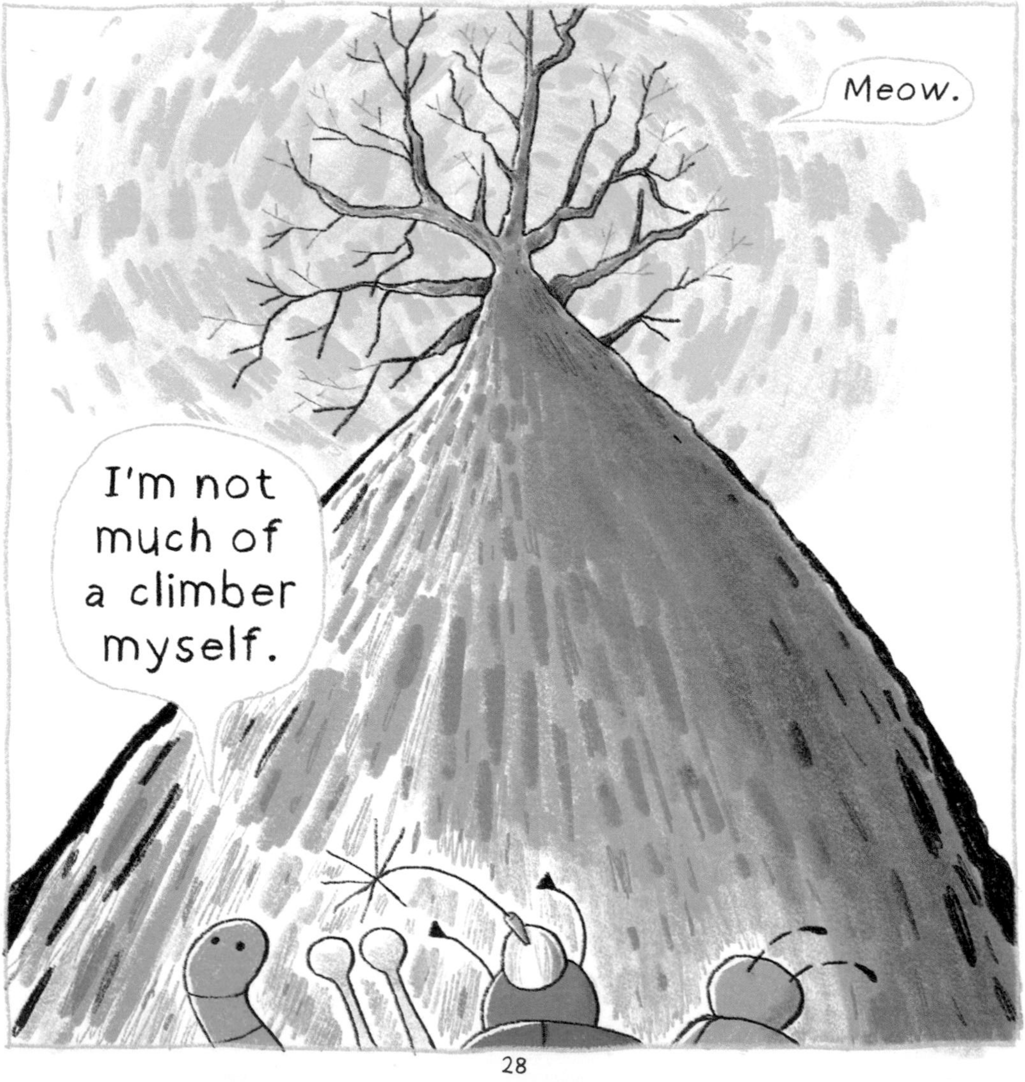
Meow.
I'm not much of a climber myself.

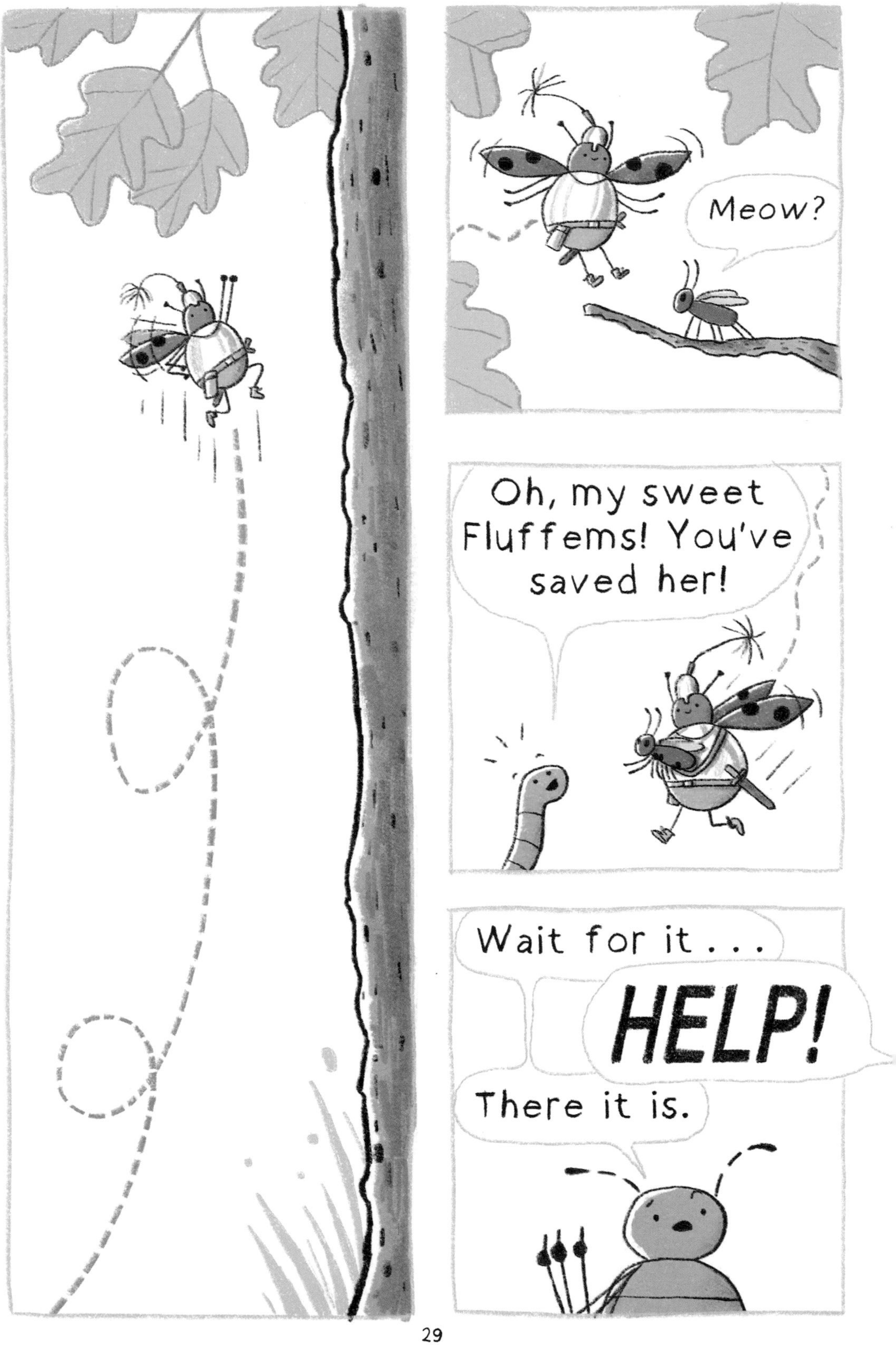
Meow?
Oh, my sweet Fluffems! You've saved her!
Wait for it . . .
HELP!
There it is.

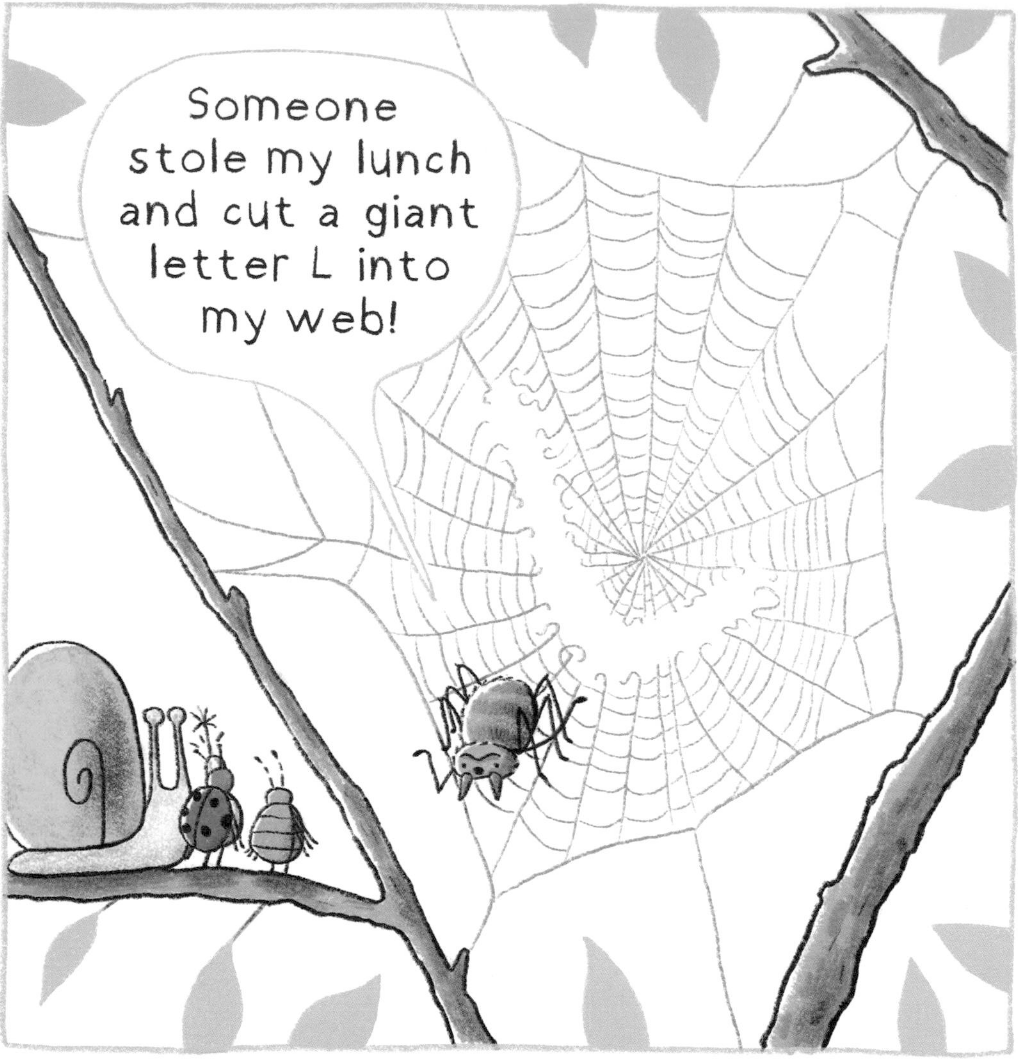
Someone stole my lunch and cut a giant letter L into my web!

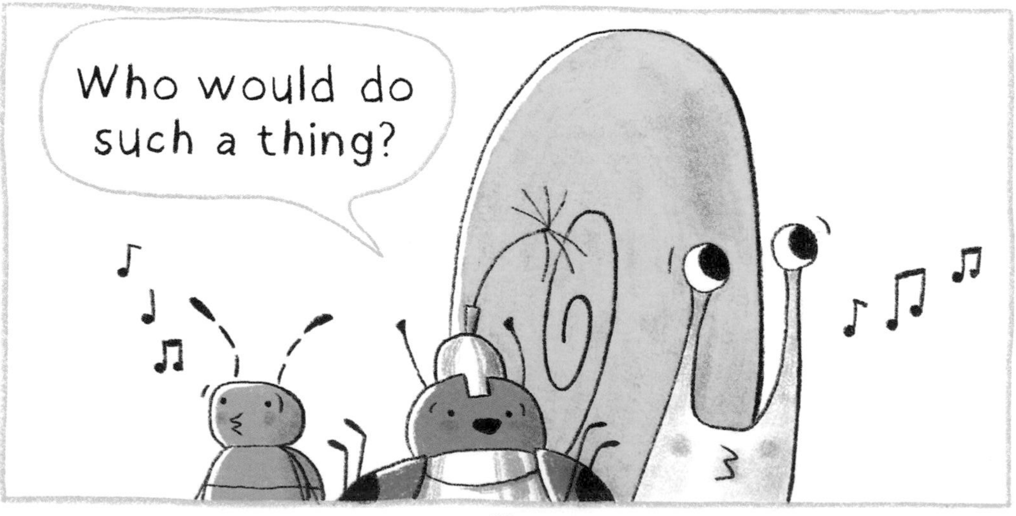
Who would do such a thing?

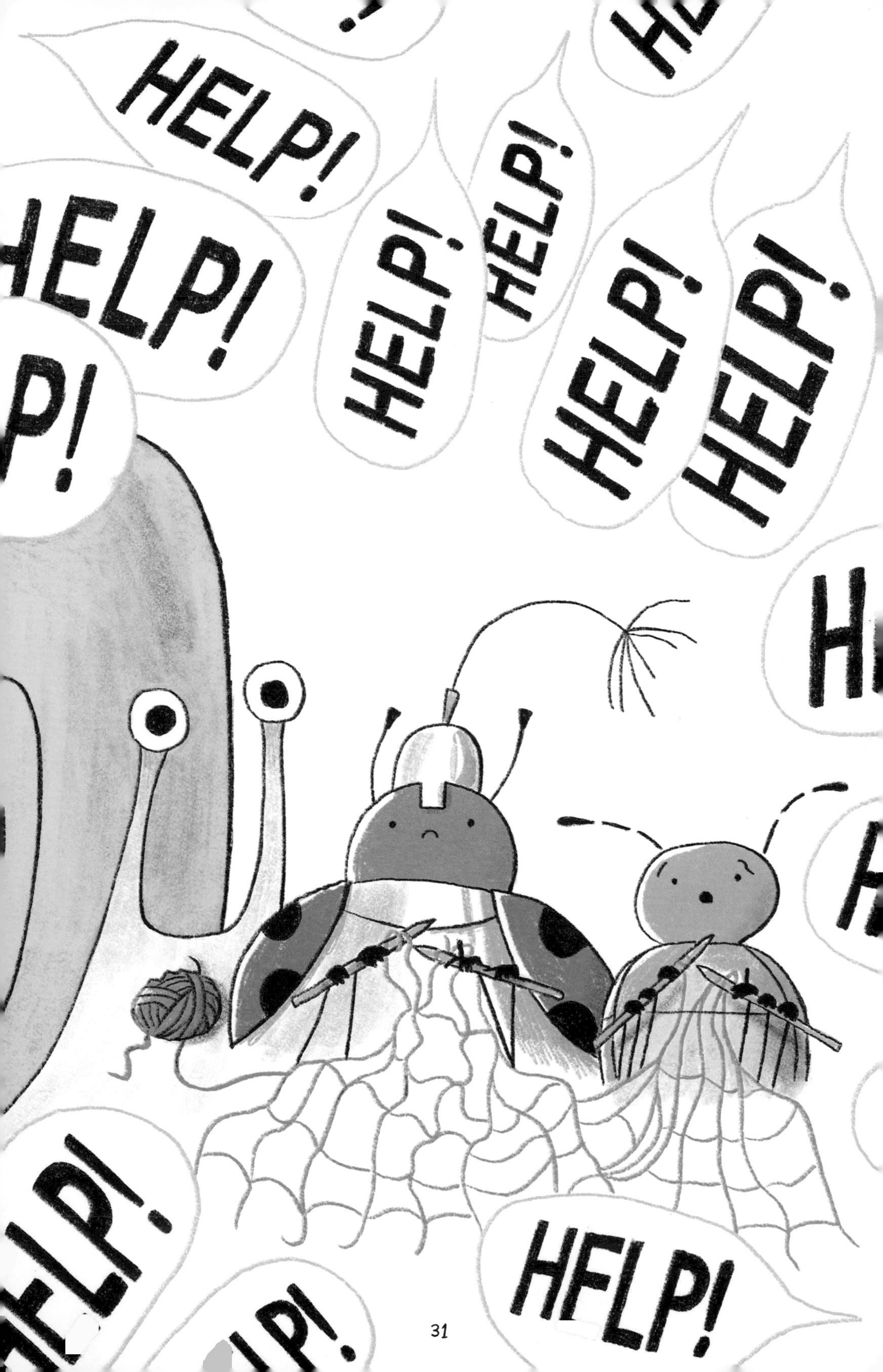
HELP!
HELP!
HELP!
HELP!
HELP!
HELP!
HFLP!

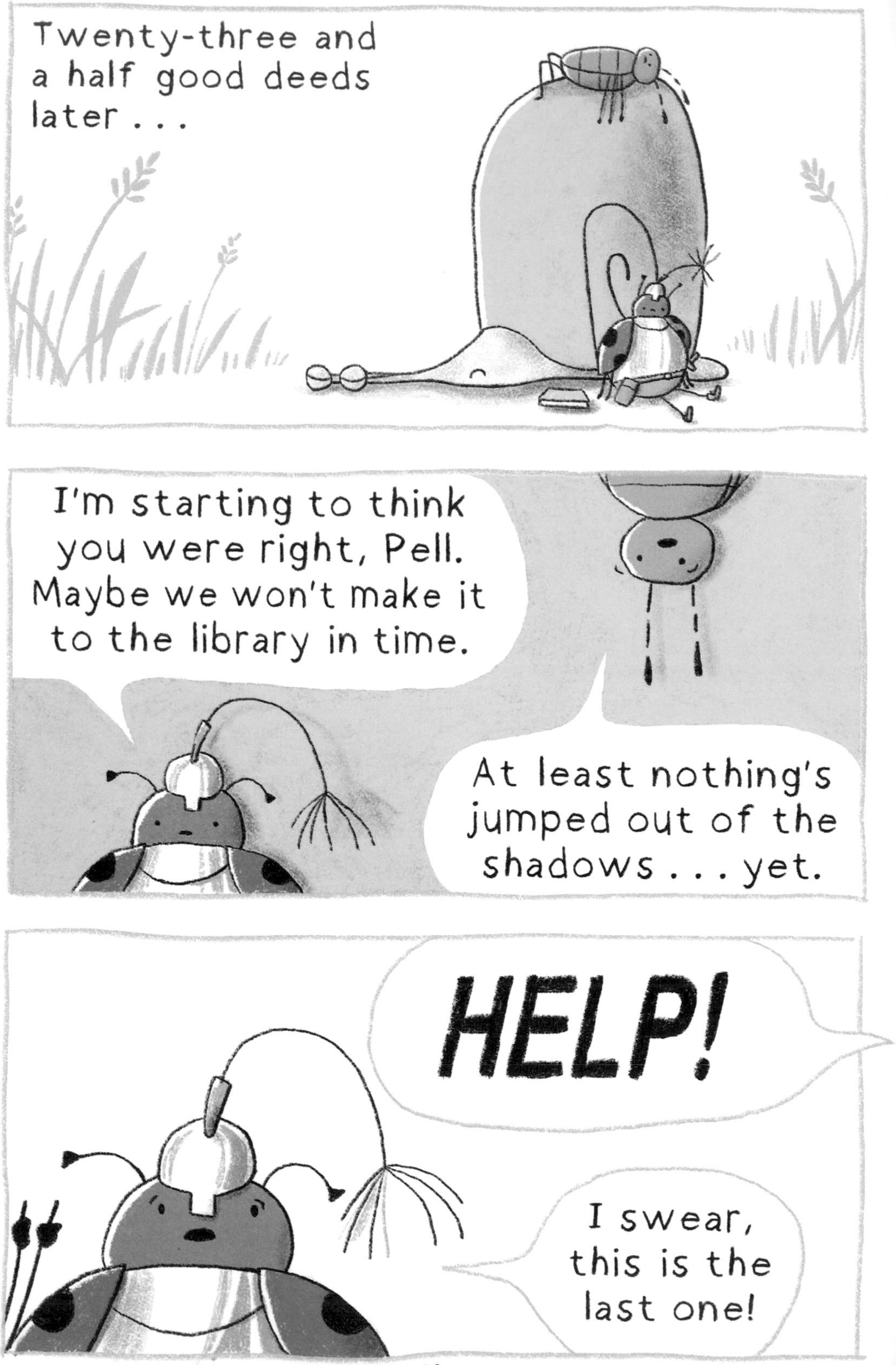
Twenty-three and a half good deeds later . . .
I'm starting to think you were right, Pell. Maybe we won't make it to the library in time.
At least nothing's jumped out of the shadows . . . yet.
HELP!
I swear, this is the last one!

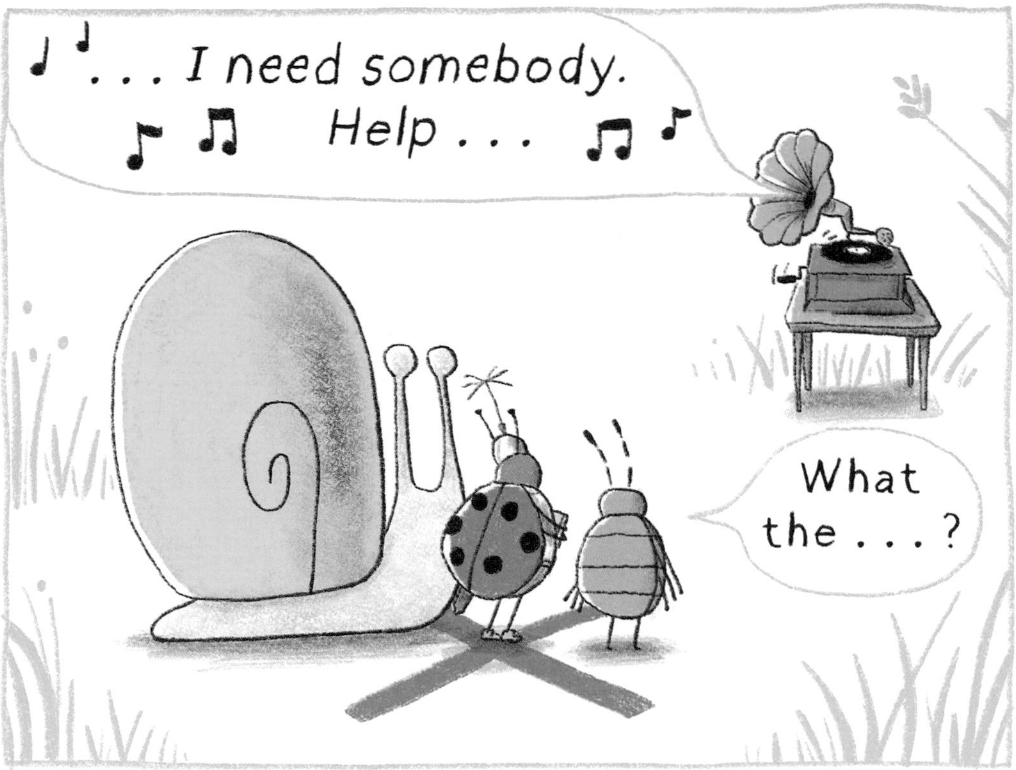
. . . I need somebody. Help . . .
What the . . . ?

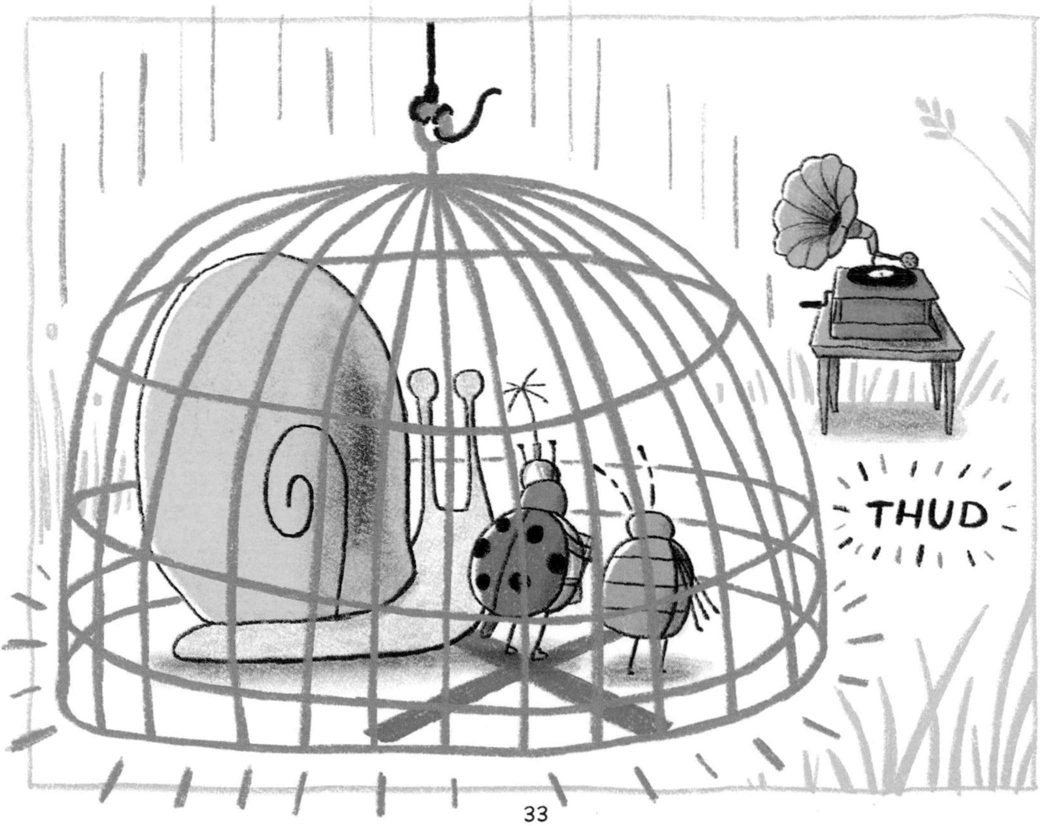
THUD

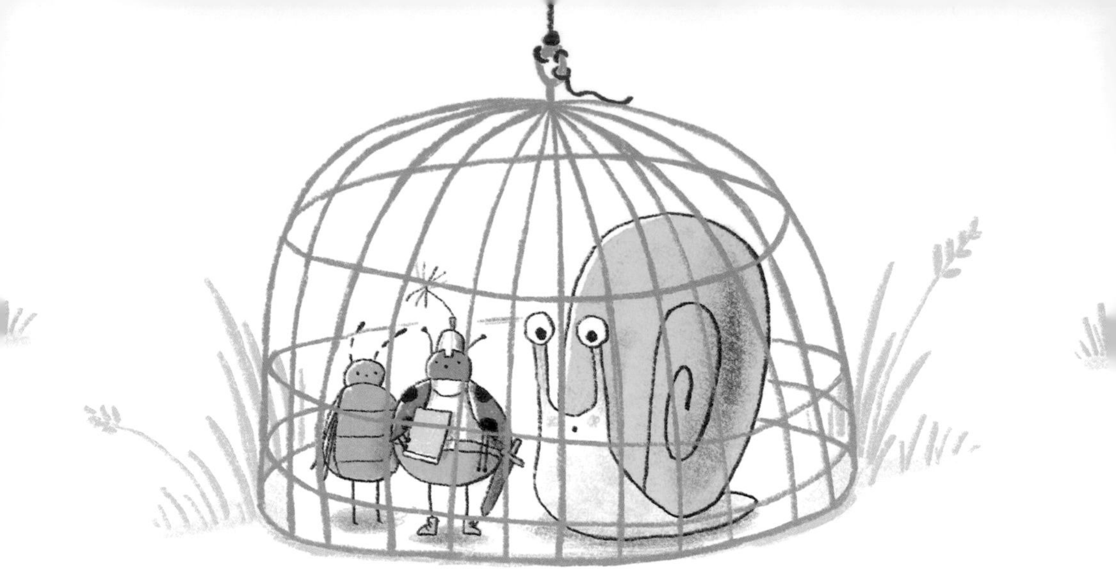

Chapter 3: The Bookworms

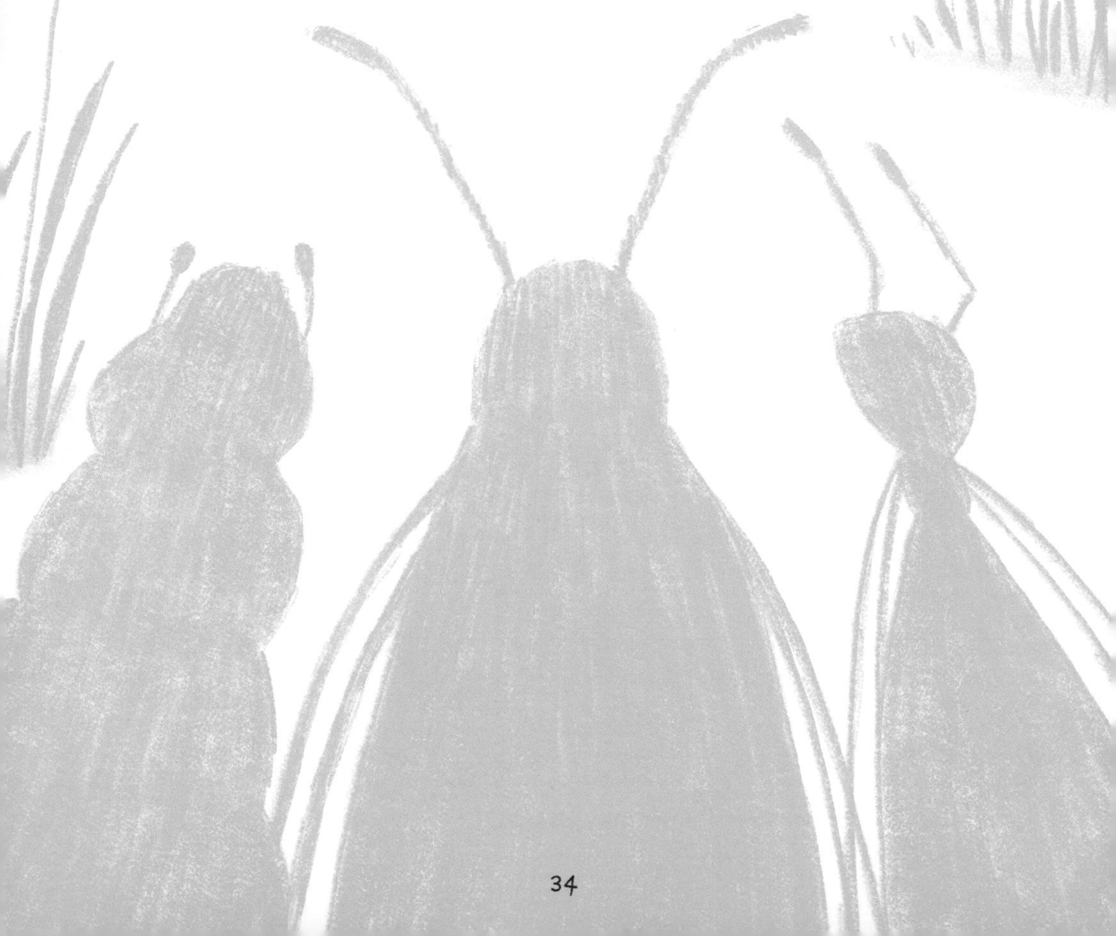

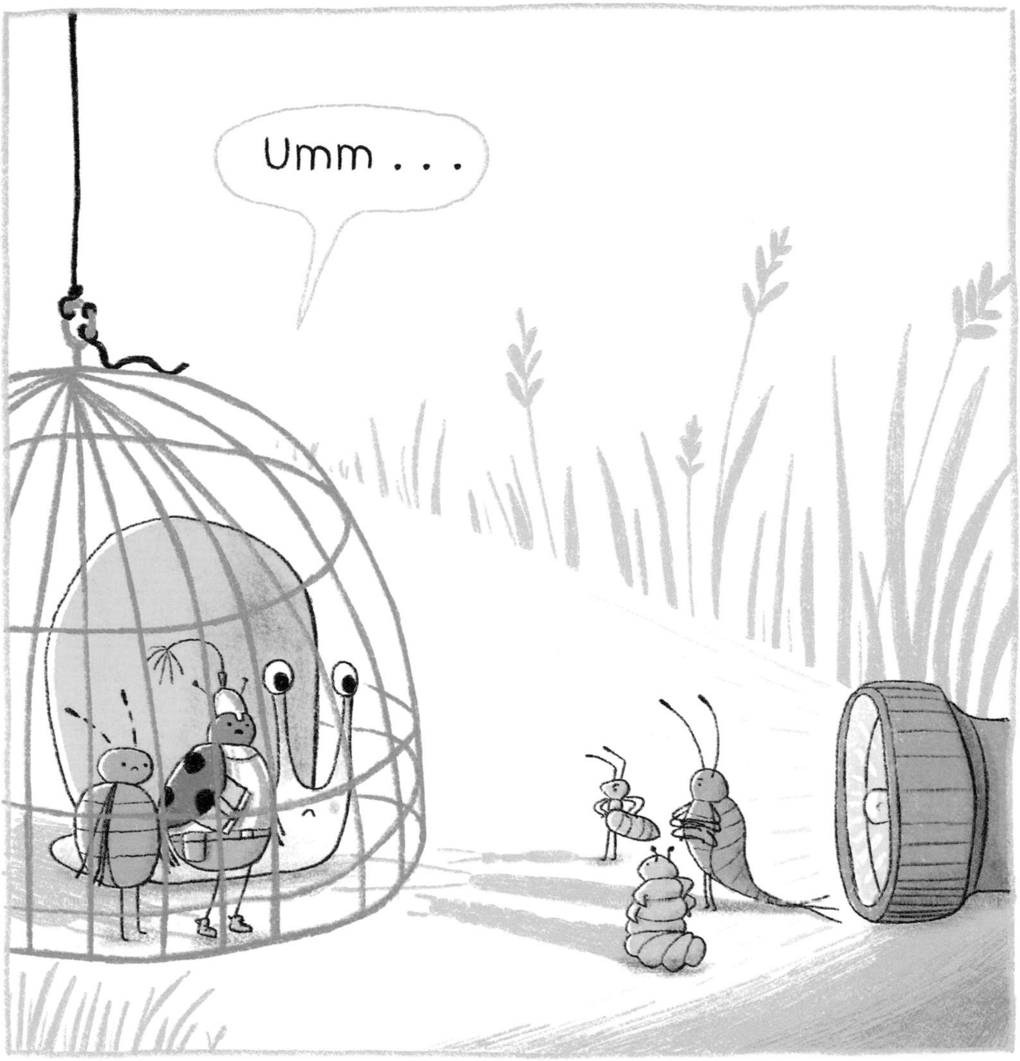
Umm . . .

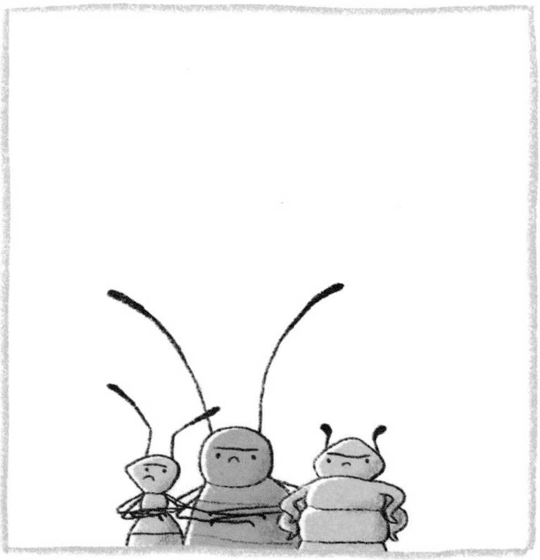

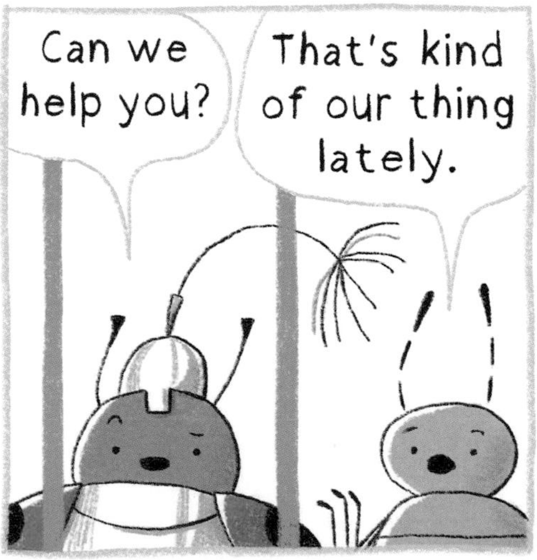
Can we help you?
That's kind of our thing lately.

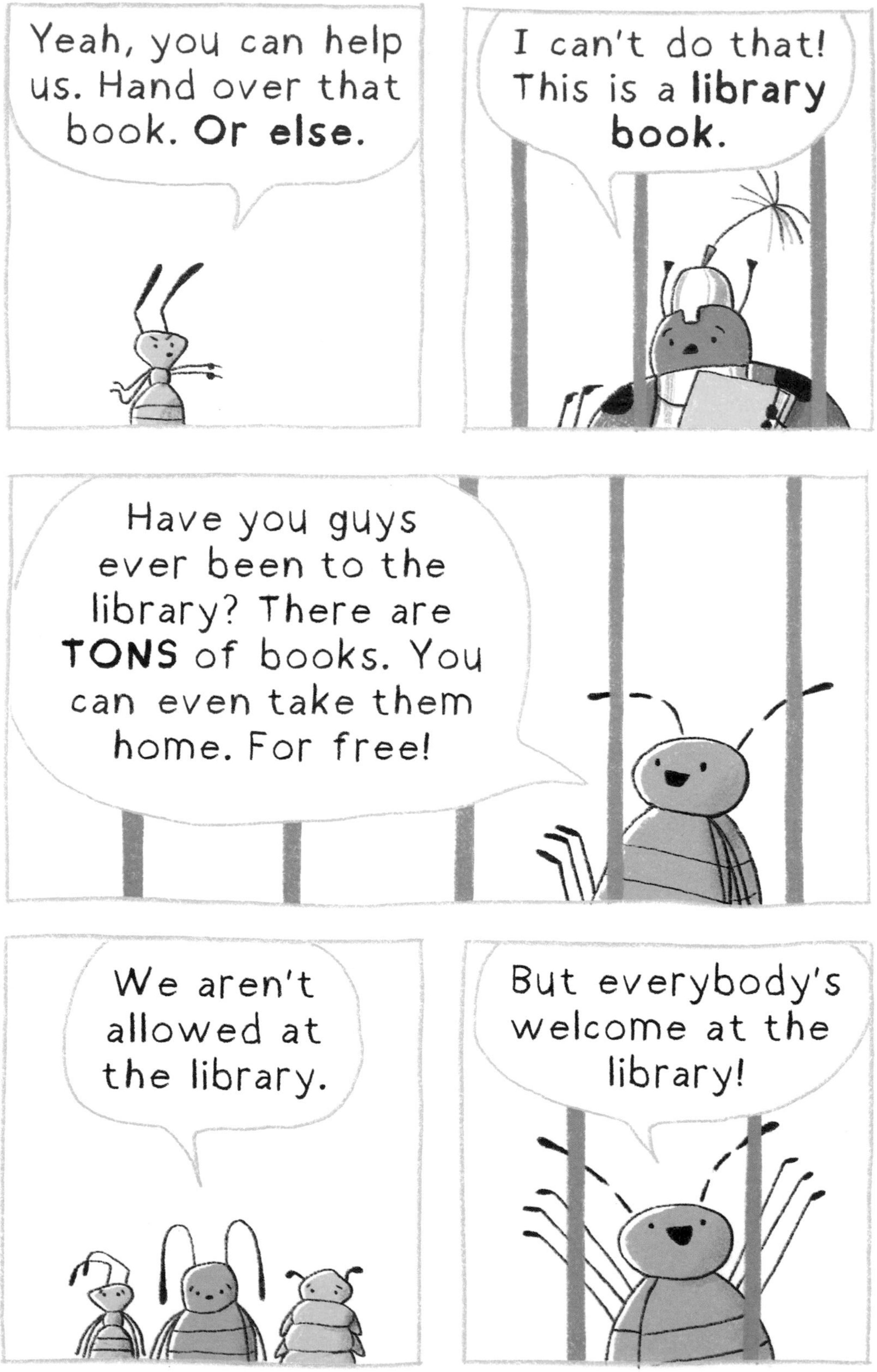
Yeah, you can help us. Hand over that book. **Or else.**
I can't do that! This is a **library book.**
Have you guys ever been to the library? There are **TONS** of books. You can even take them home. For free!
We aren't allowed at the library.
But everybody's welcome at the library!

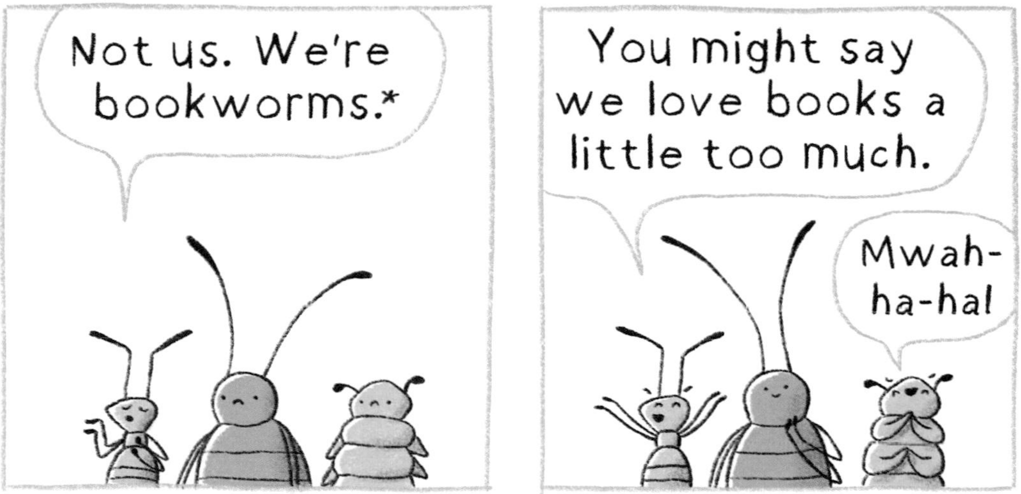
Not us. We're bookworms.*
You might say we love books a little too much.
Mwah-ha-ha!

*__bookworms__: book-loving insects like book lice, silverfish, and beetle larvae

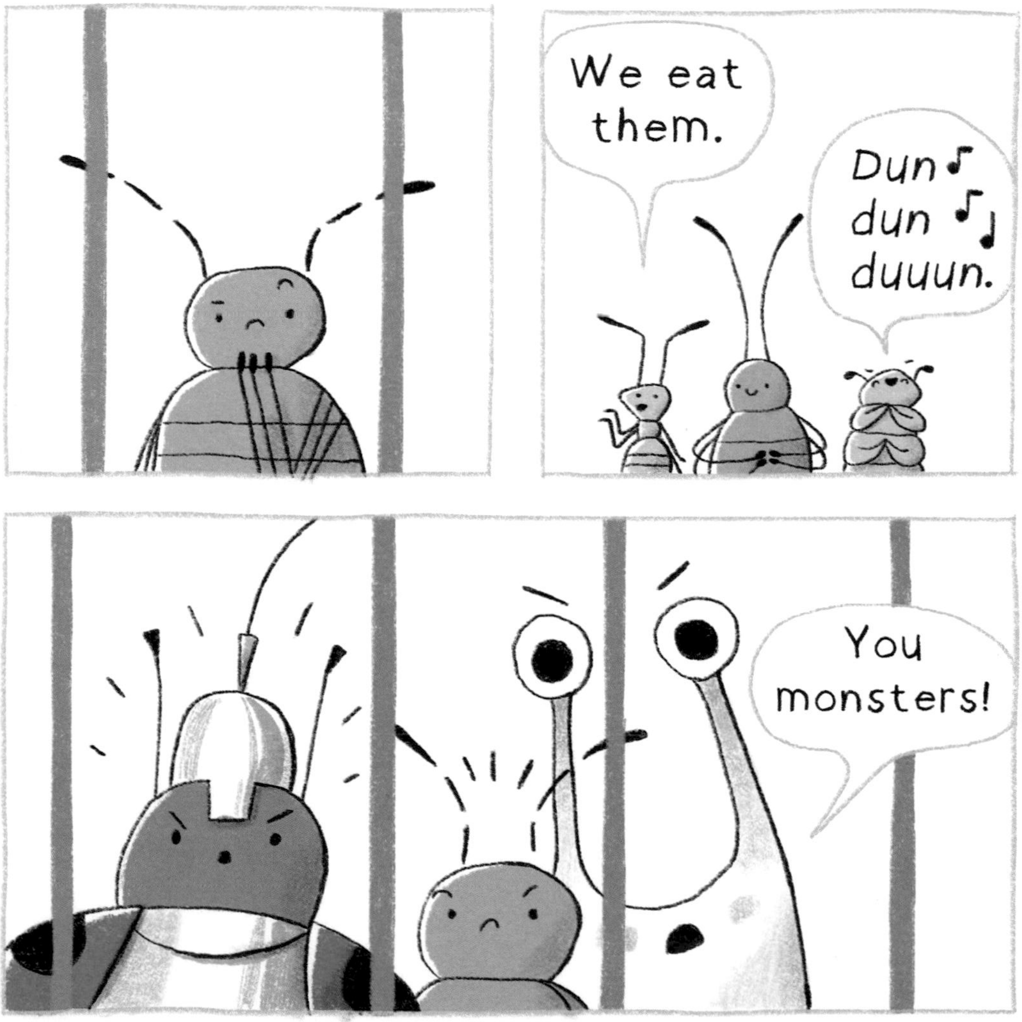
We eat them.
Dun ♪ dun ♪♩ duuun.
You monsters!

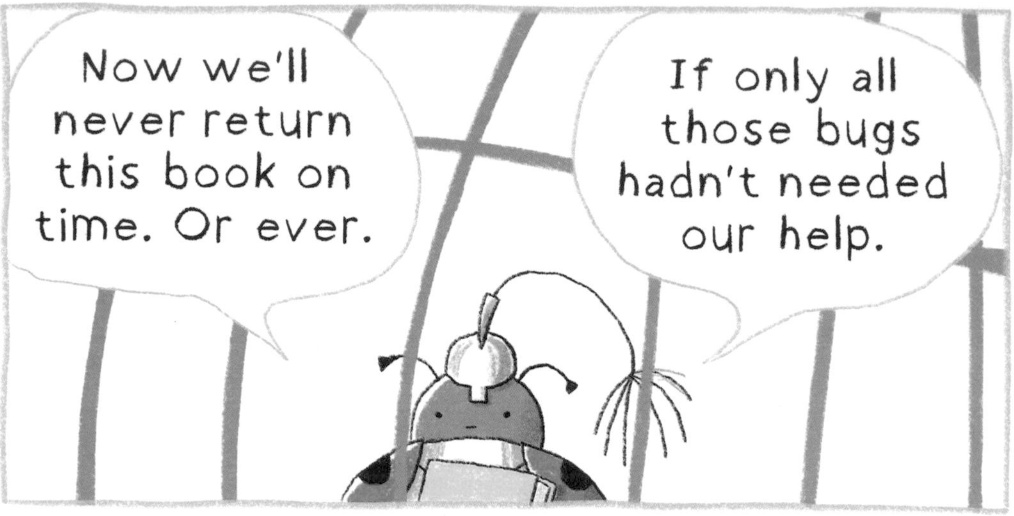
Now we'll never return this book on time. Or ever.
If only all those bugs hadn't needed our help.

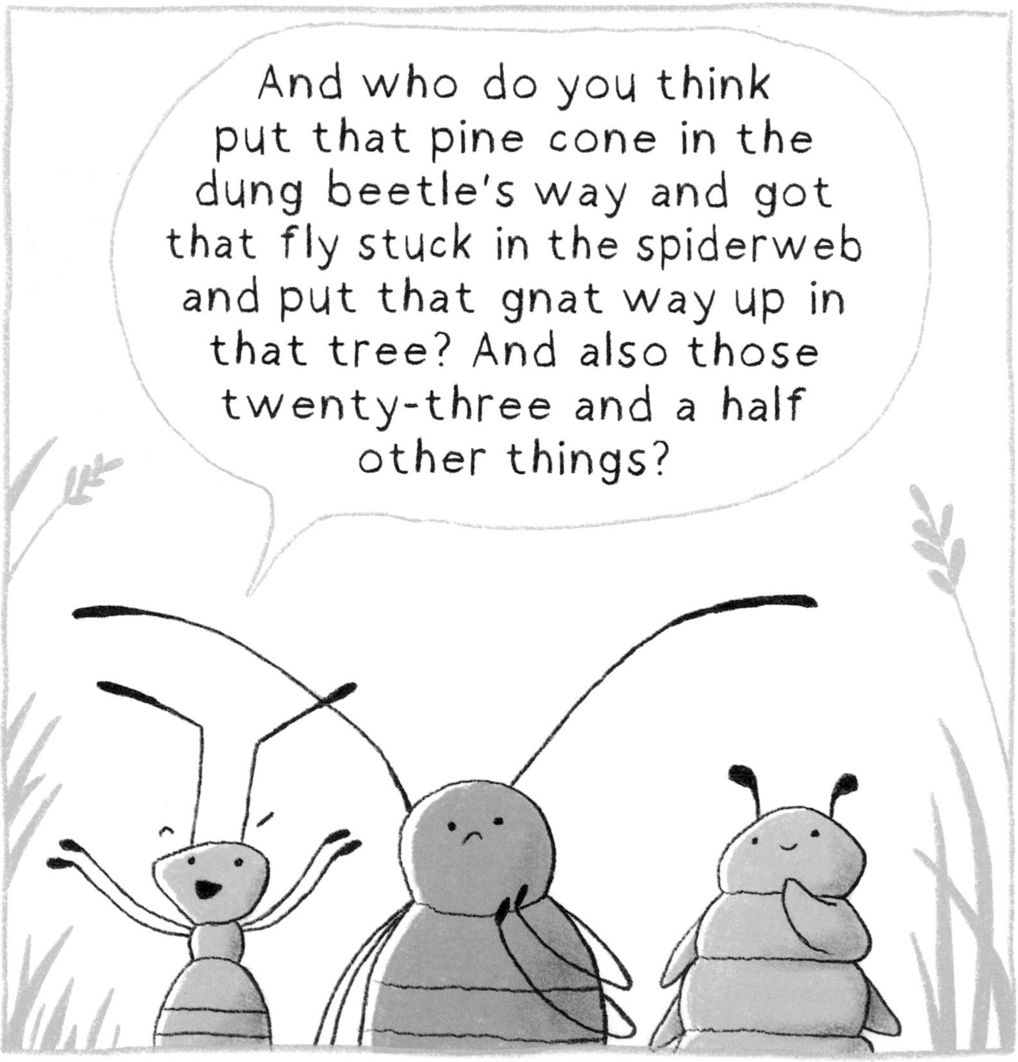
And who do you think put that pine cone in the dung beetle's way and got that fly stuck in the spiderweb and put that gnat way up in that tree? And also those twenty-three and a half other things?

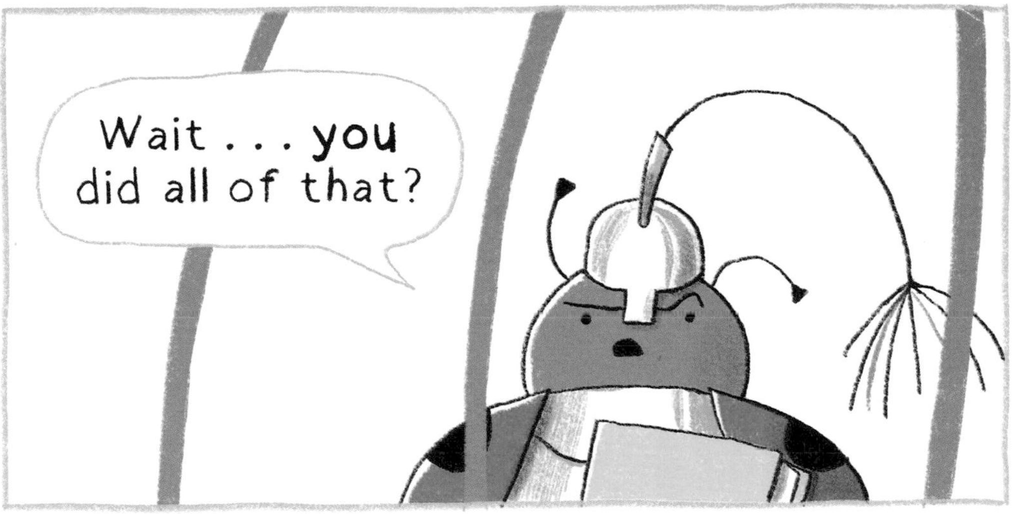
Wait . . . **you** did all of that?

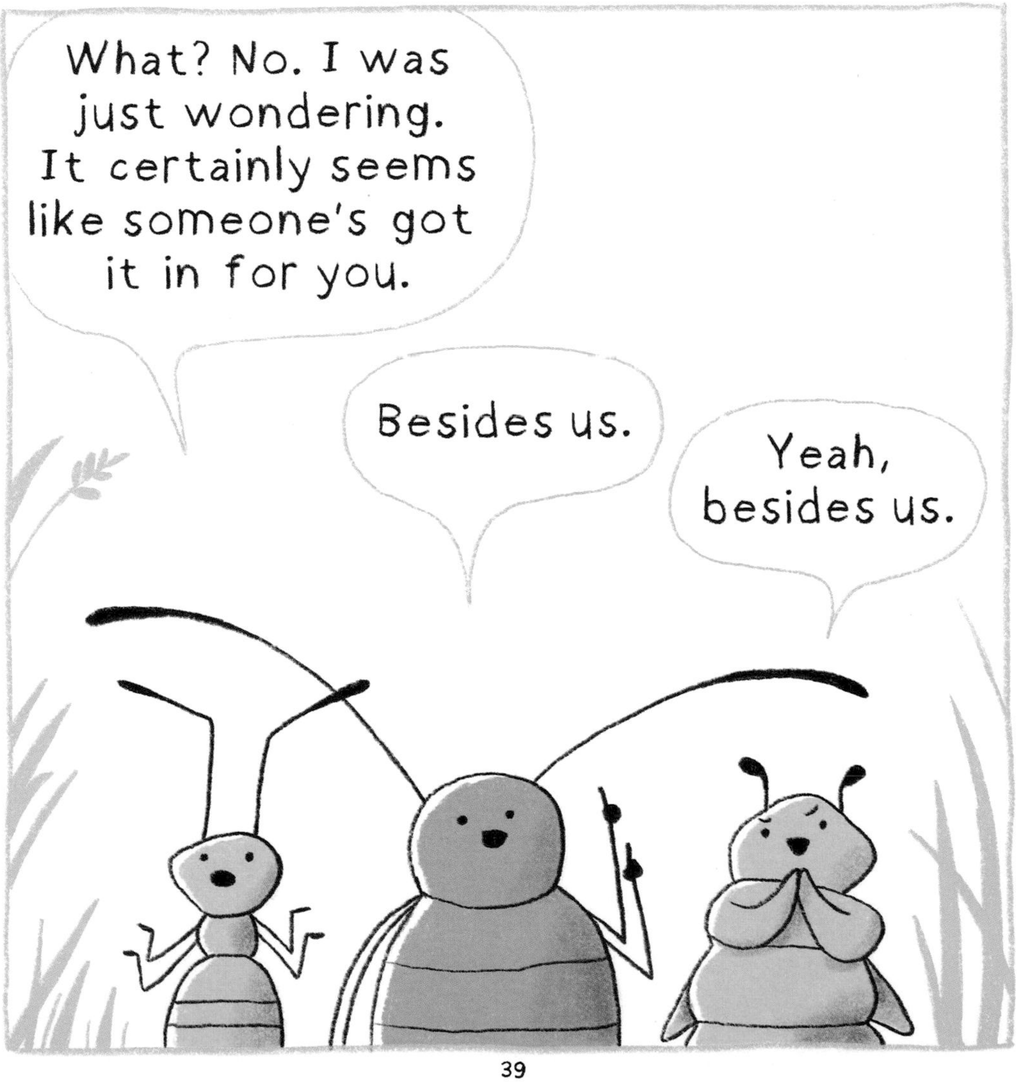
What? No. I was just wondering. It certainly seems like someone's got it in for you.
Besides us.
Yeah, besides us.

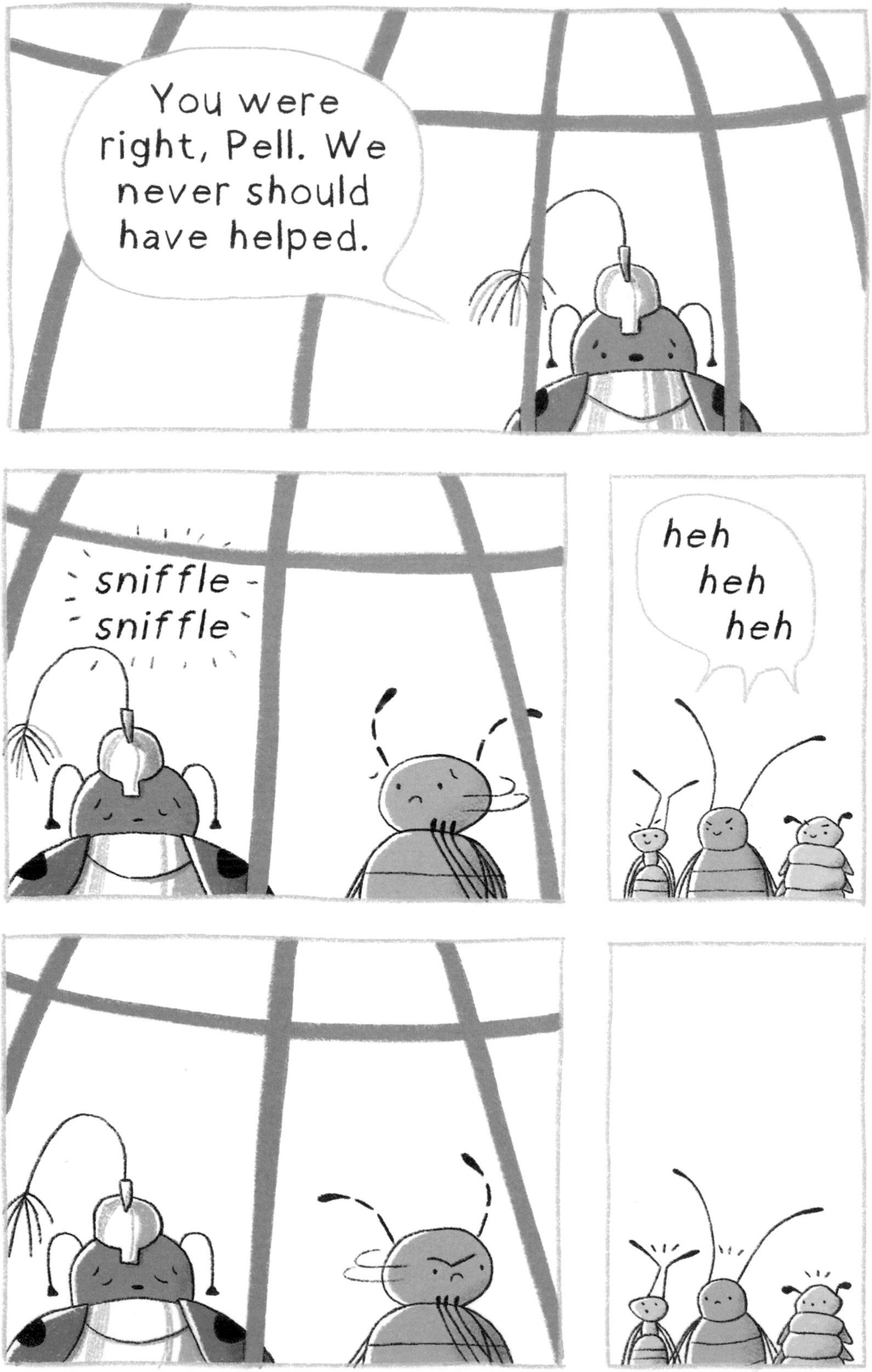
You were right, Pell. We never should have helped.
sniffle sniffle
heh heh heh

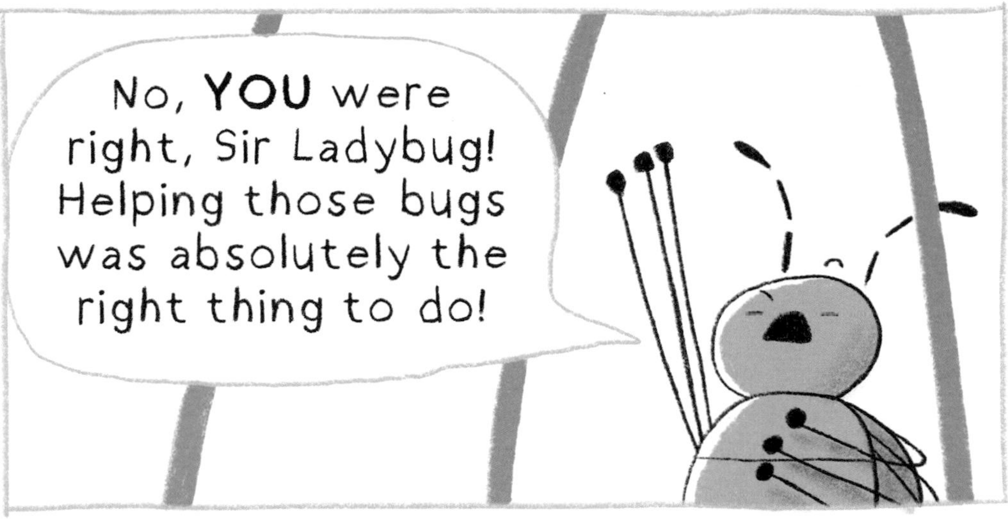
No, **YOU** were right, Sir Ladybug! Helping those bugs was absolutely the right thing to do!

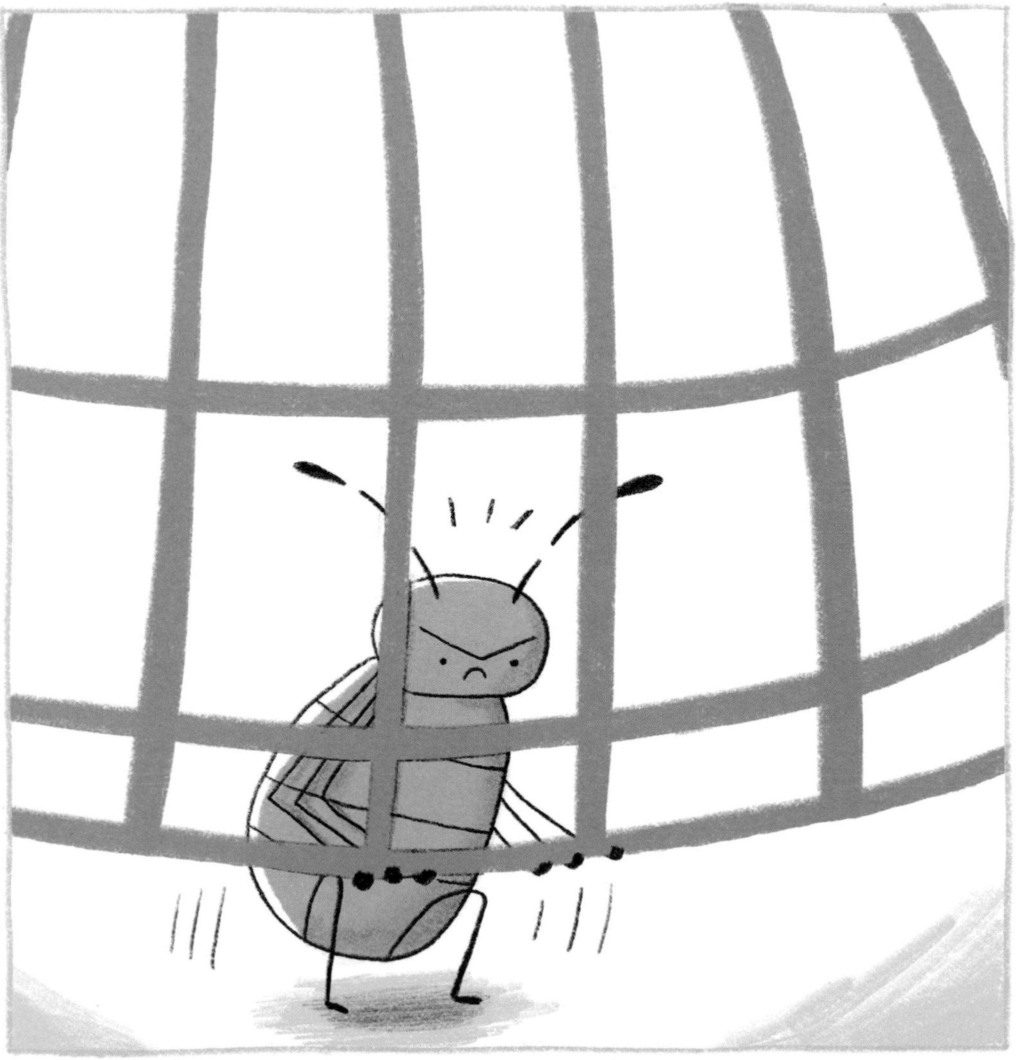

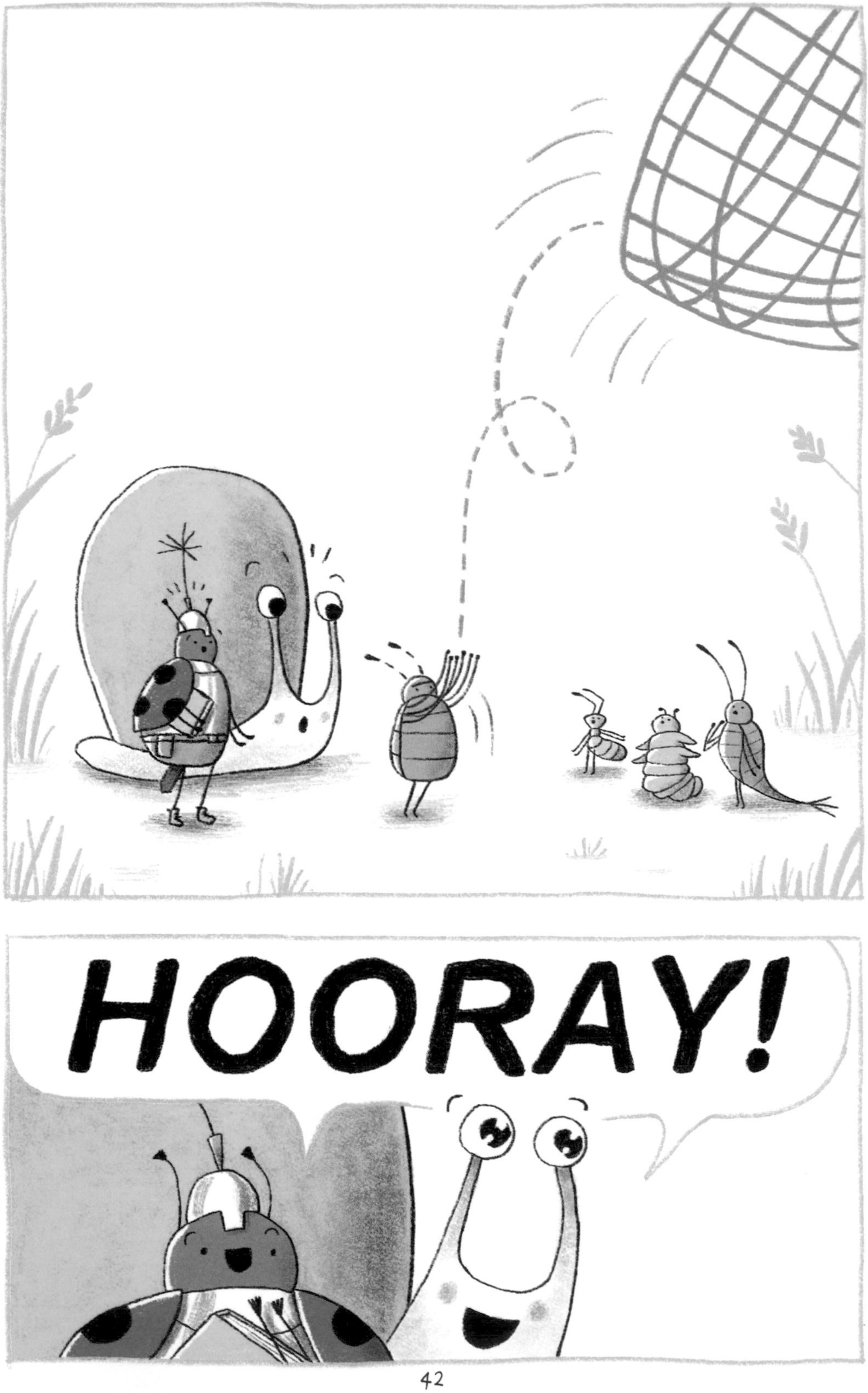
HOORAY!

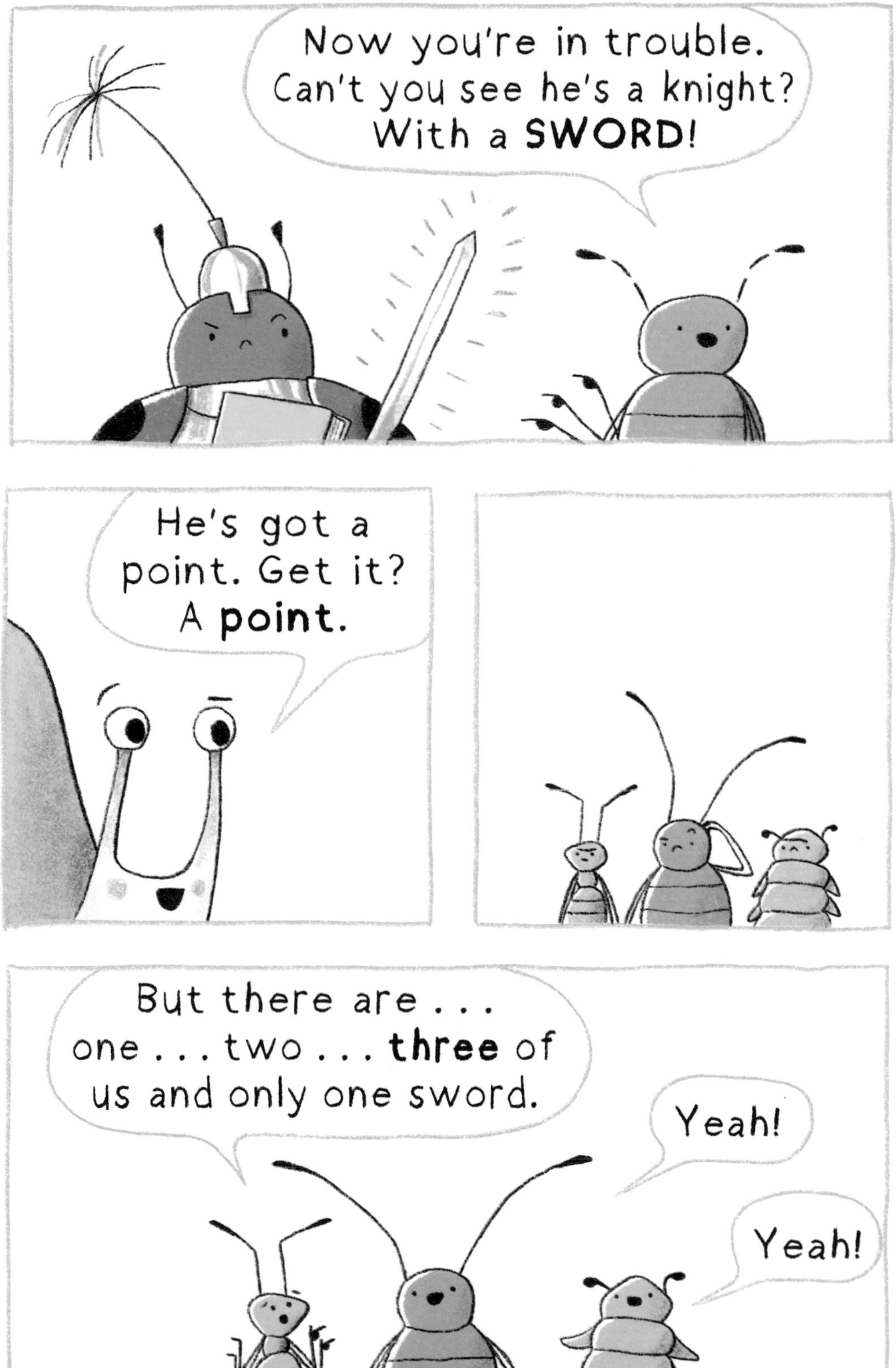
Now you're in trouble.
Can't you see he's a knight?
With a **SWORD**!
He's got a
point. Get it?
A **point**.
But there are . . .
one . . . two . . . **three** of
us and only one sword.
Yeah!
Yeah!

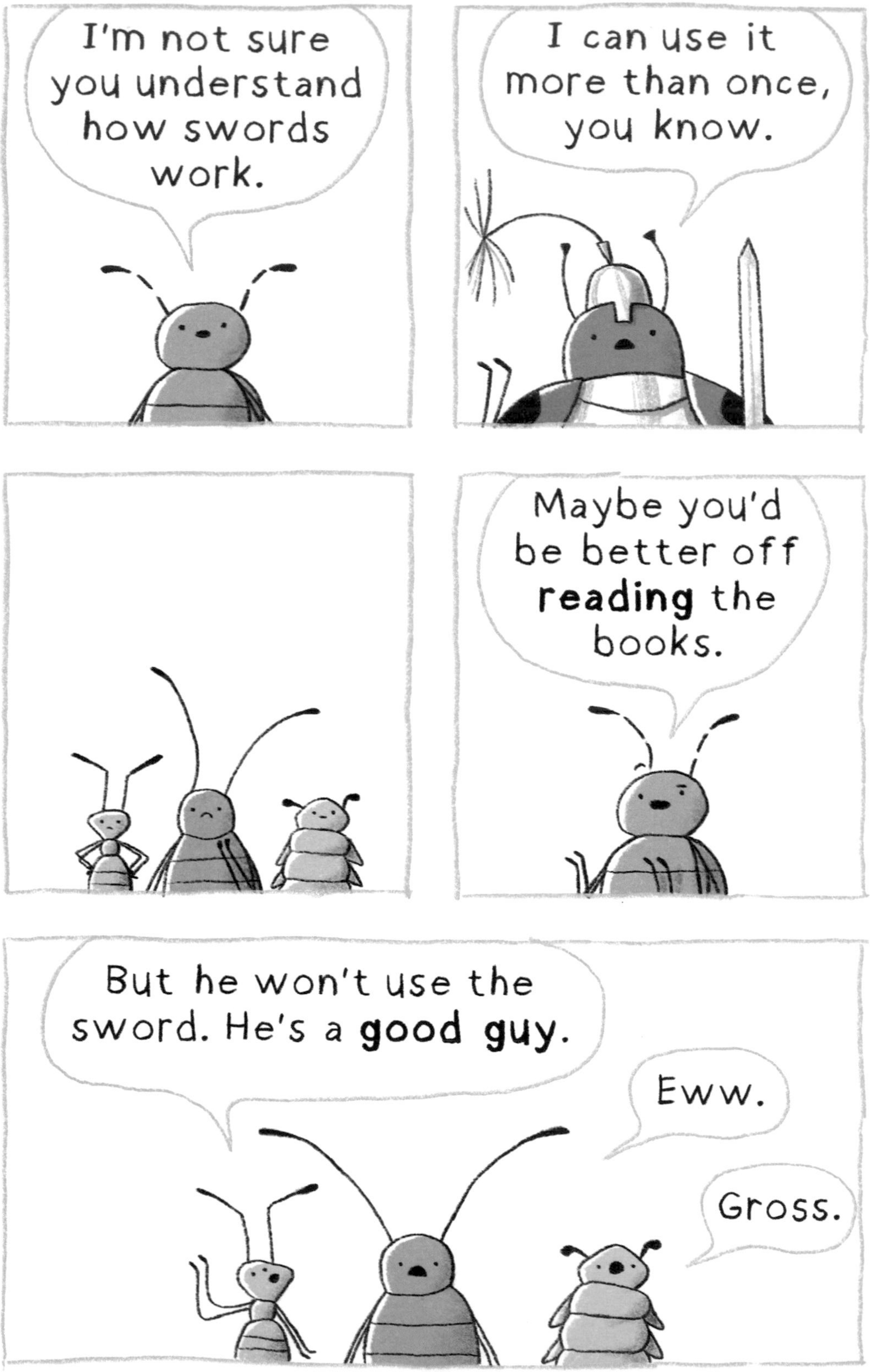

I'm not sure you understand how swords work.
I can use it more than once, you know.
Maybe you'd be better off **reading** the books.
But he won't use the sword. He's a **good guy**.
Eww.
Gross.

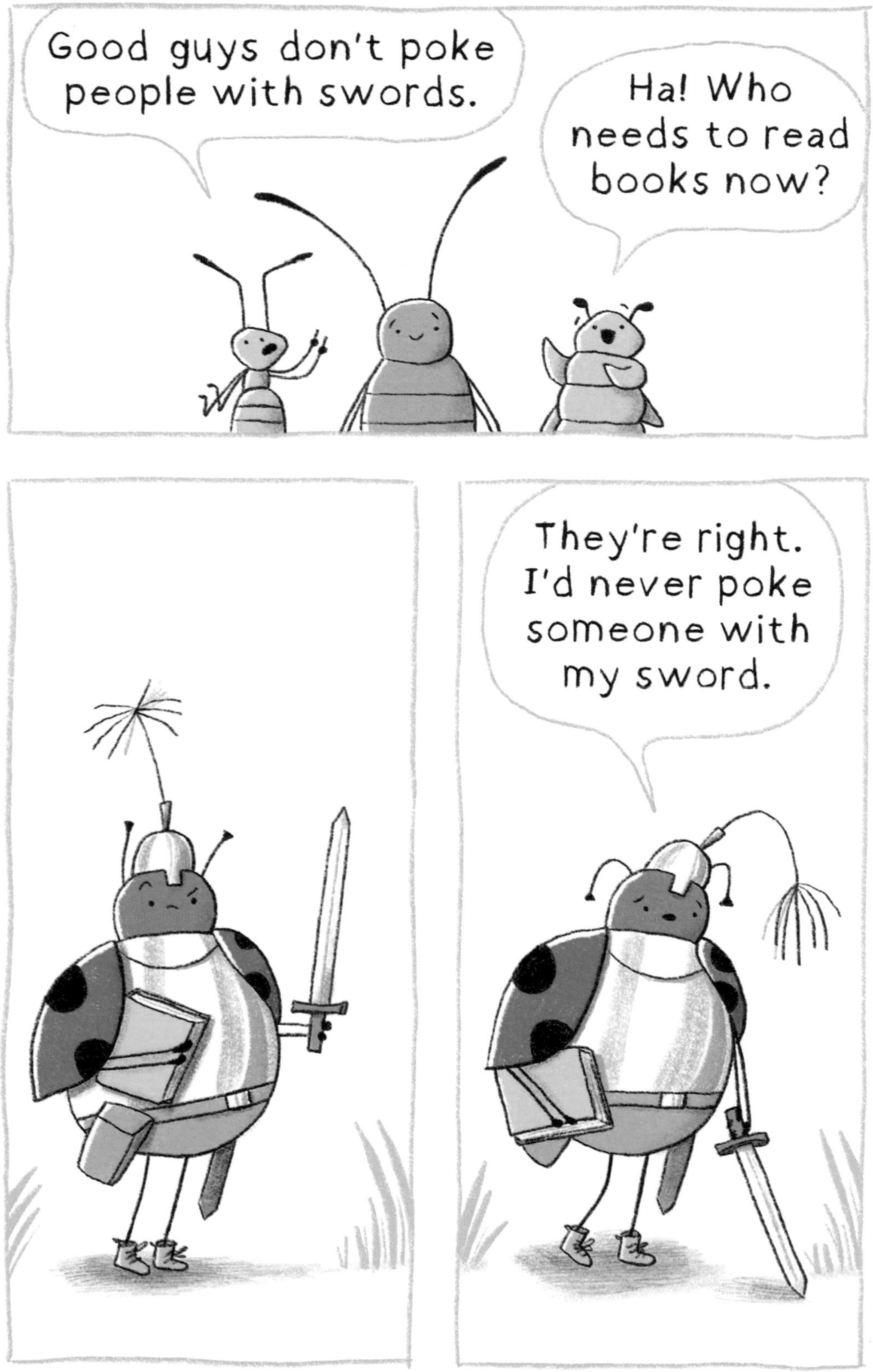

Good guys don't poke people with swords.
Ha! Who needs to read books now?
They're right. I'd never poke someone with my sword.

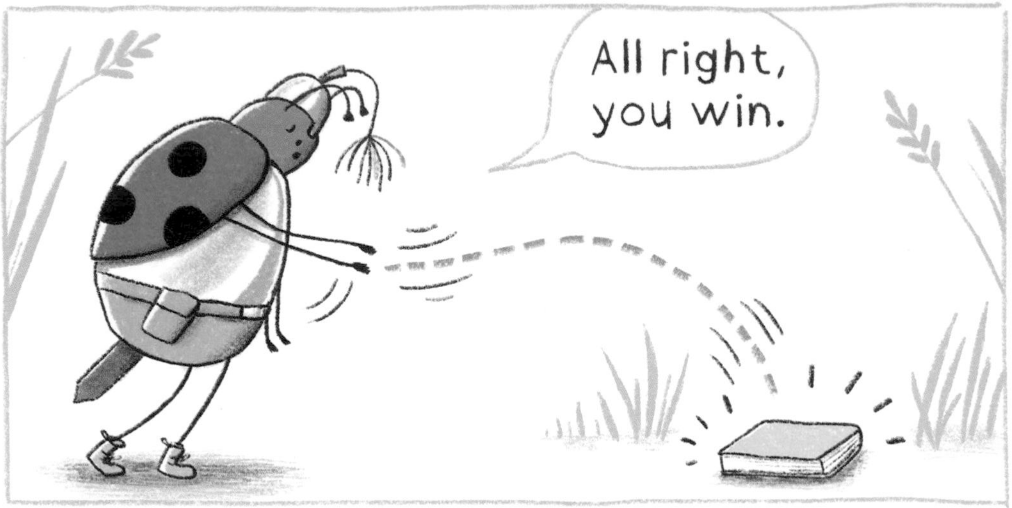
All right, you win.

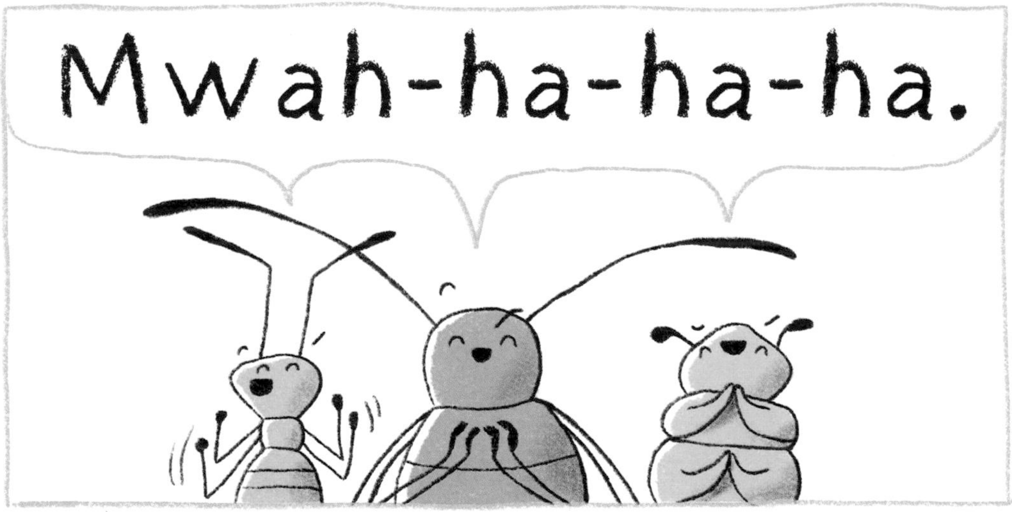
Mwah-ha-ha-ha.

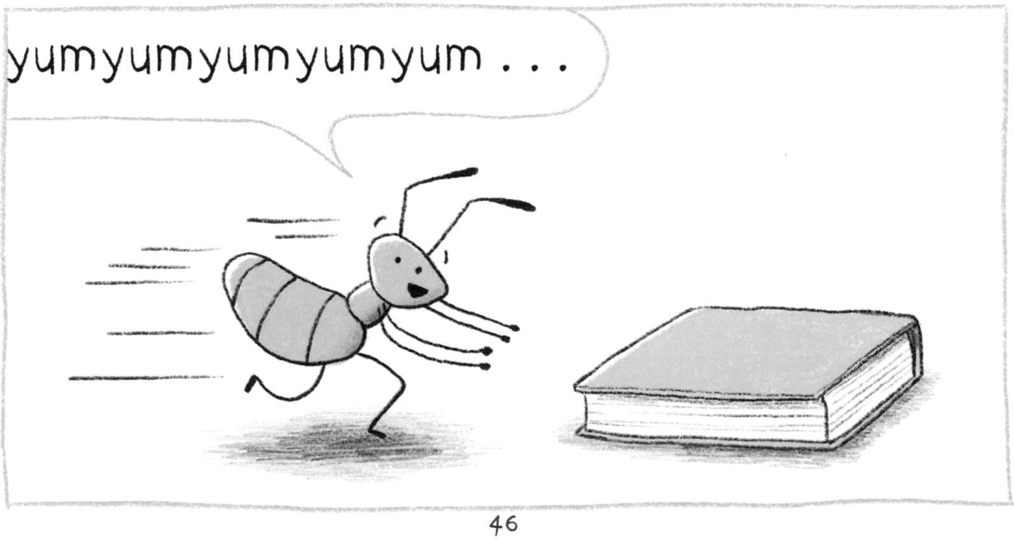
yumyumyumyumyum . . .

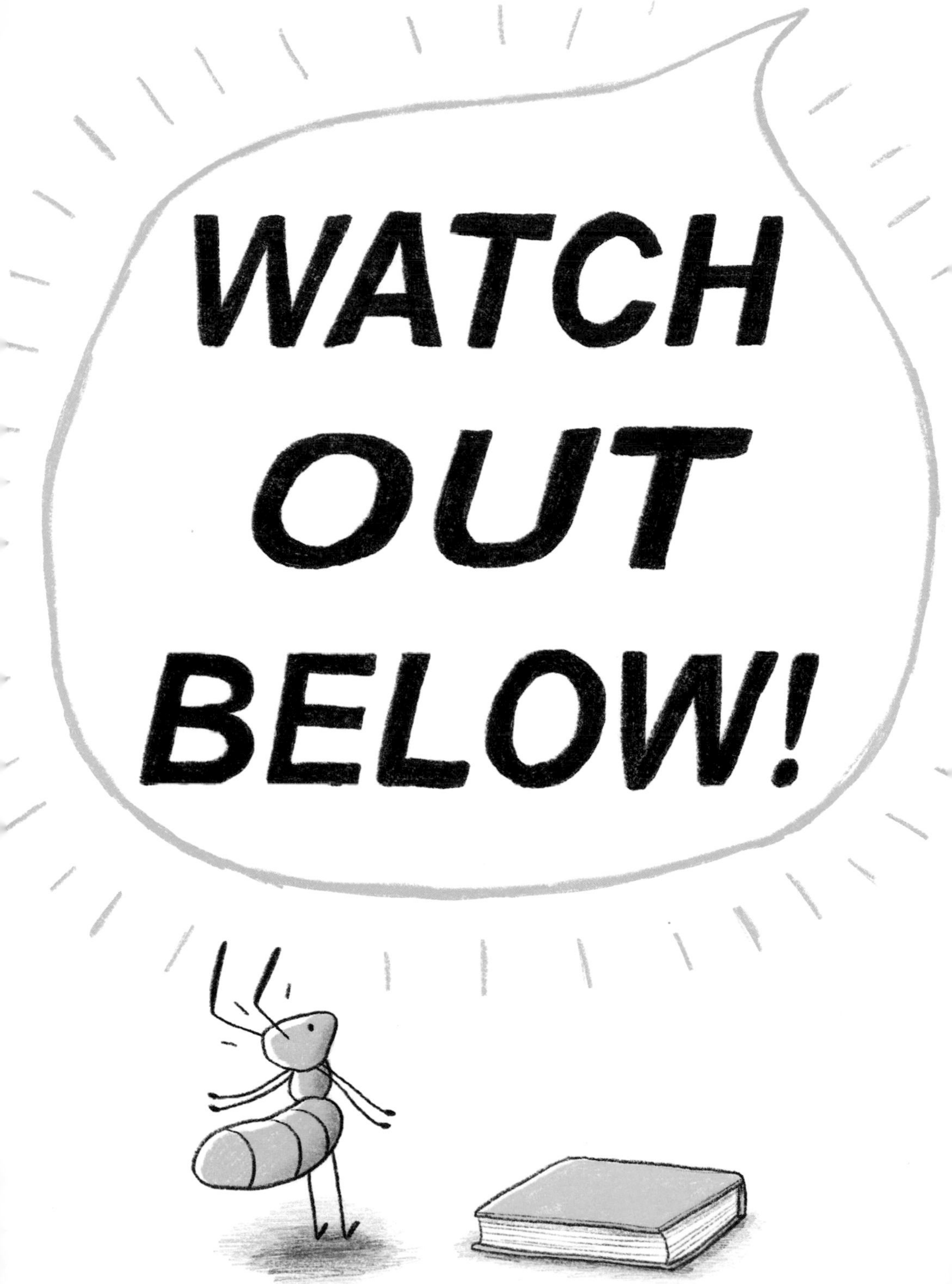
WATCH OUT BELOW!

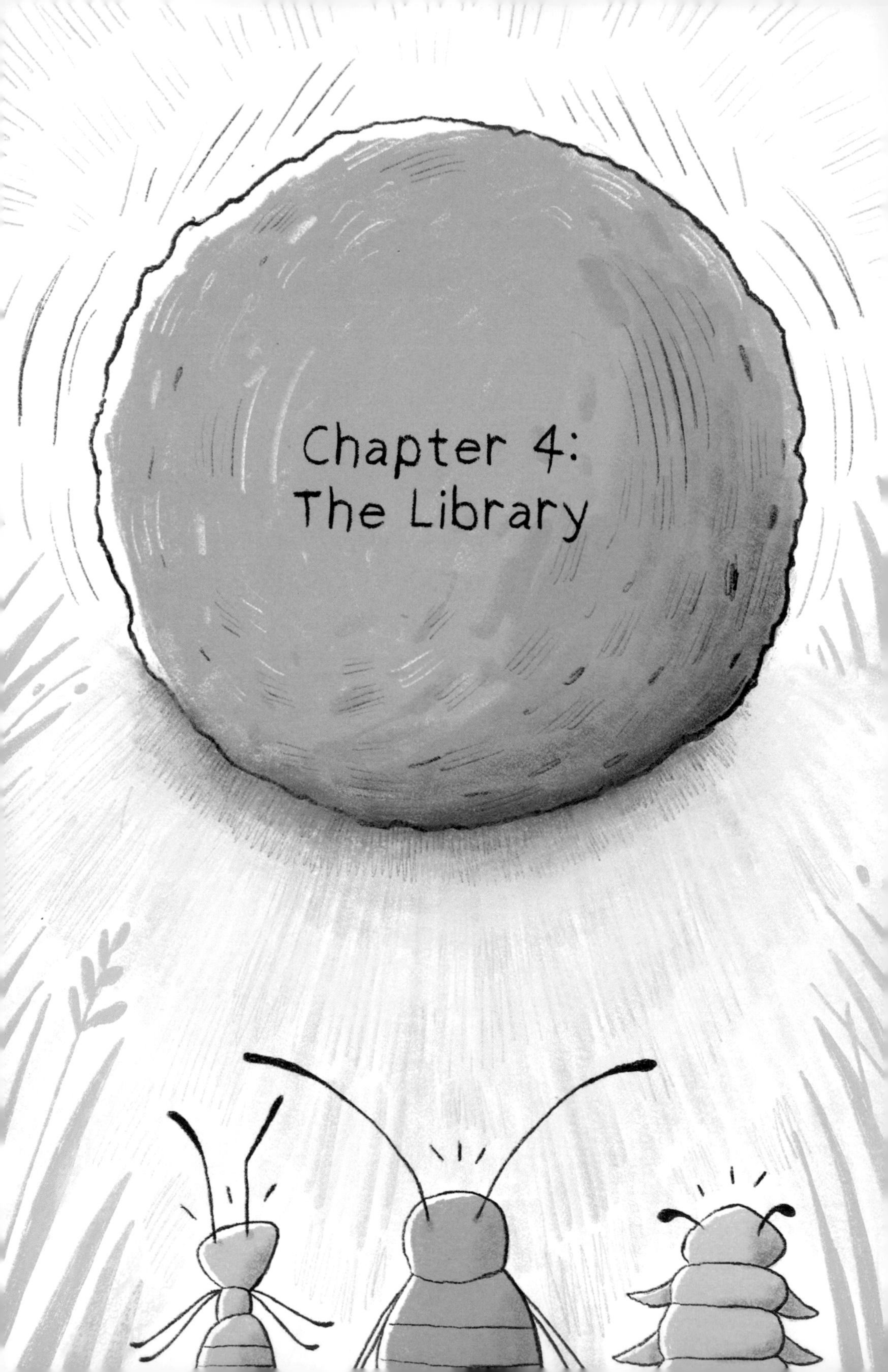
Chapter 4:
The Library

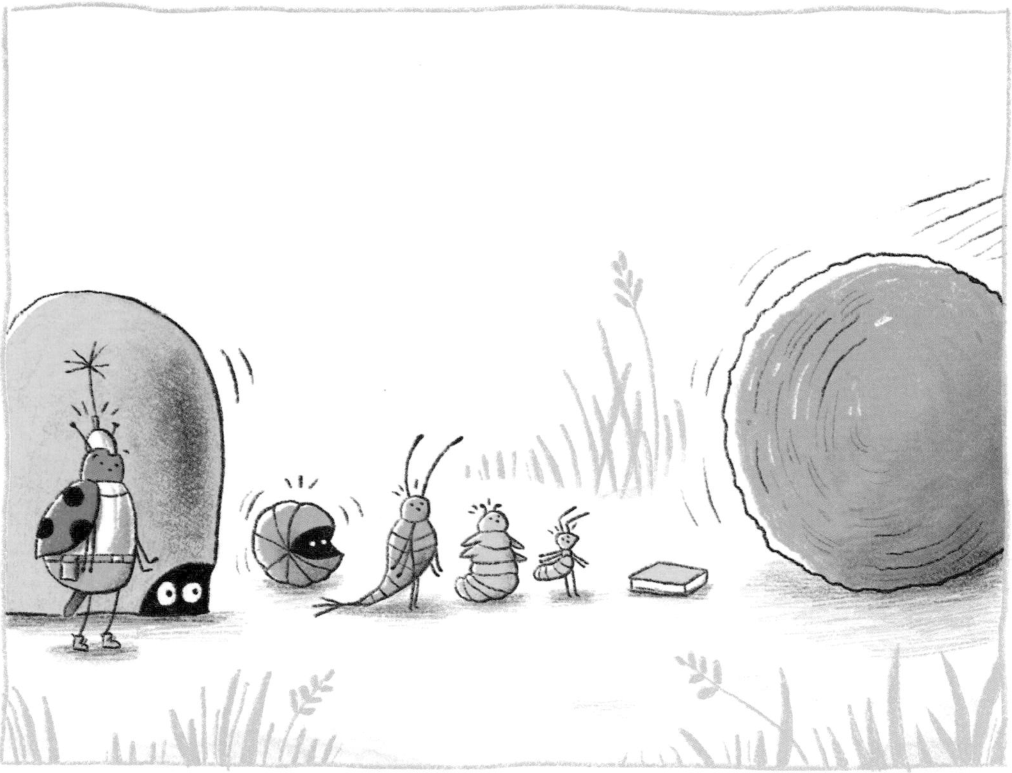

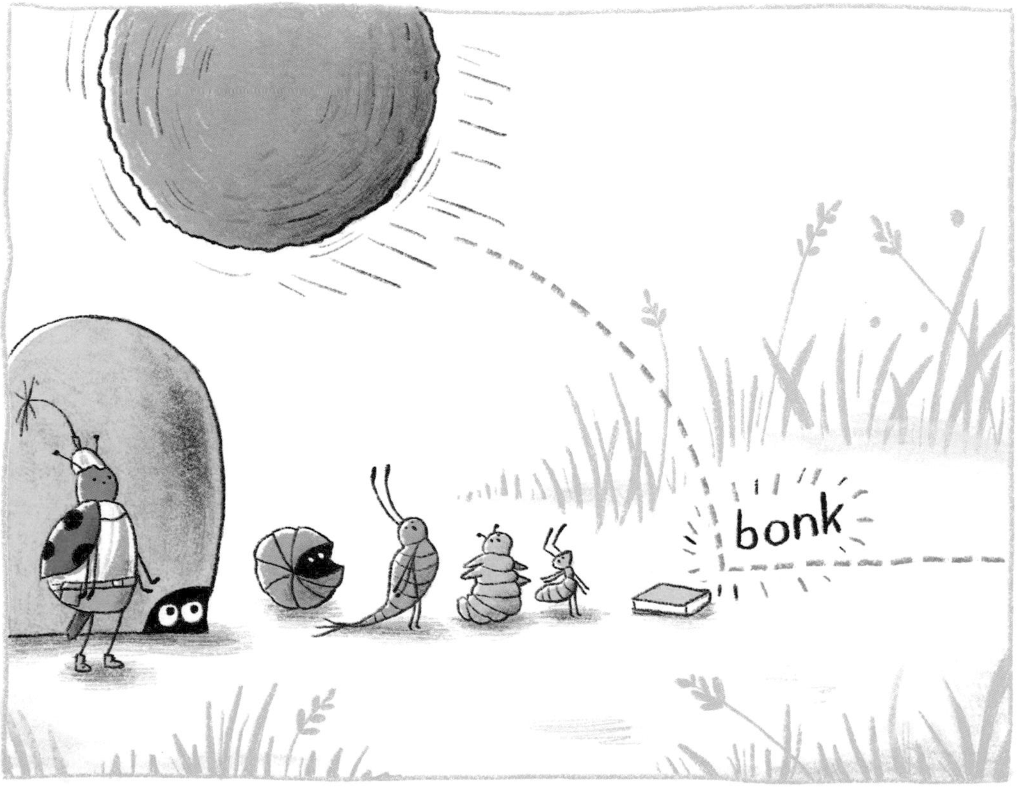
bonk

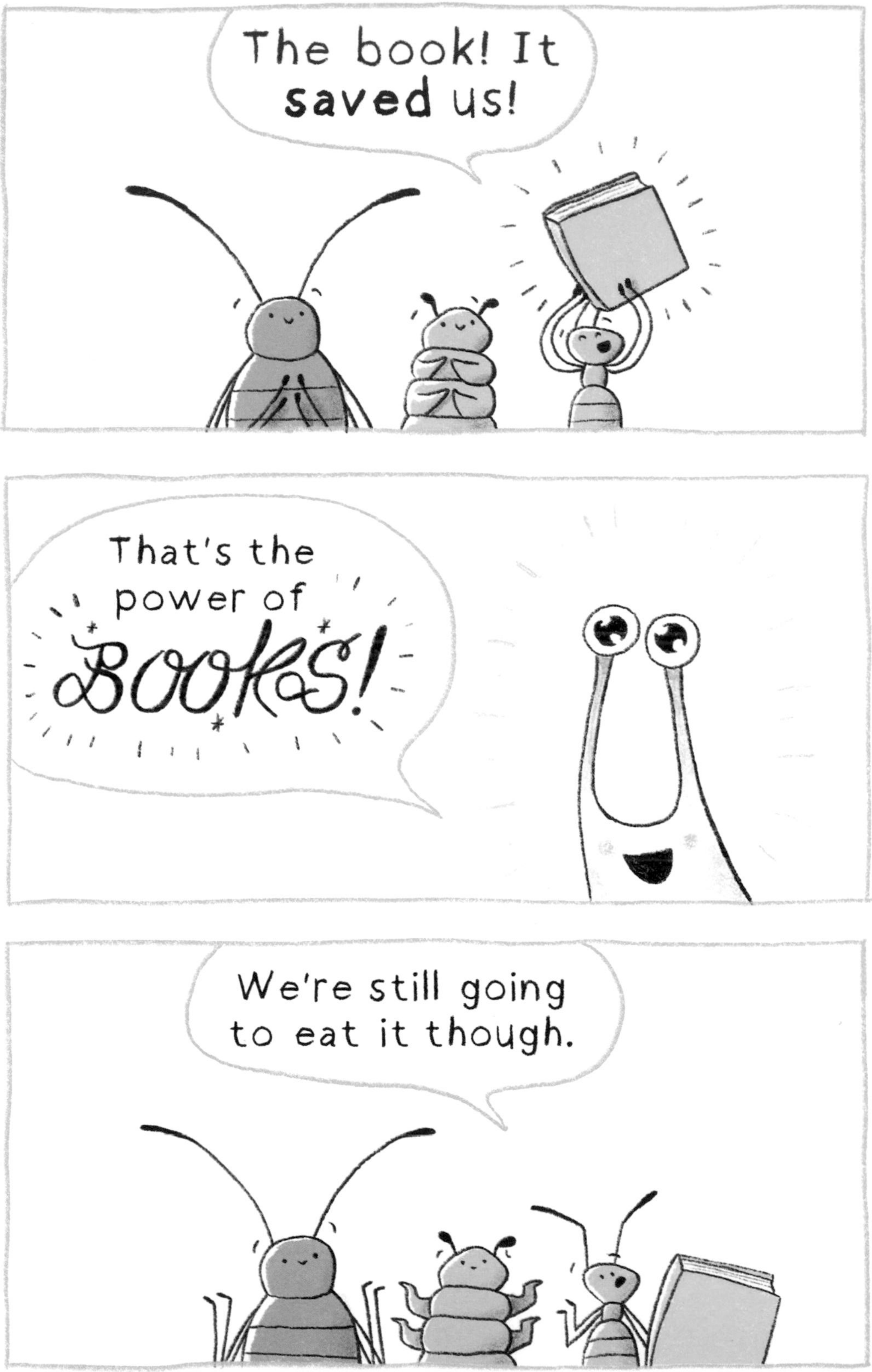
The book! It saved us!
That's the power of BOOKS!
We're still going to eat it though.

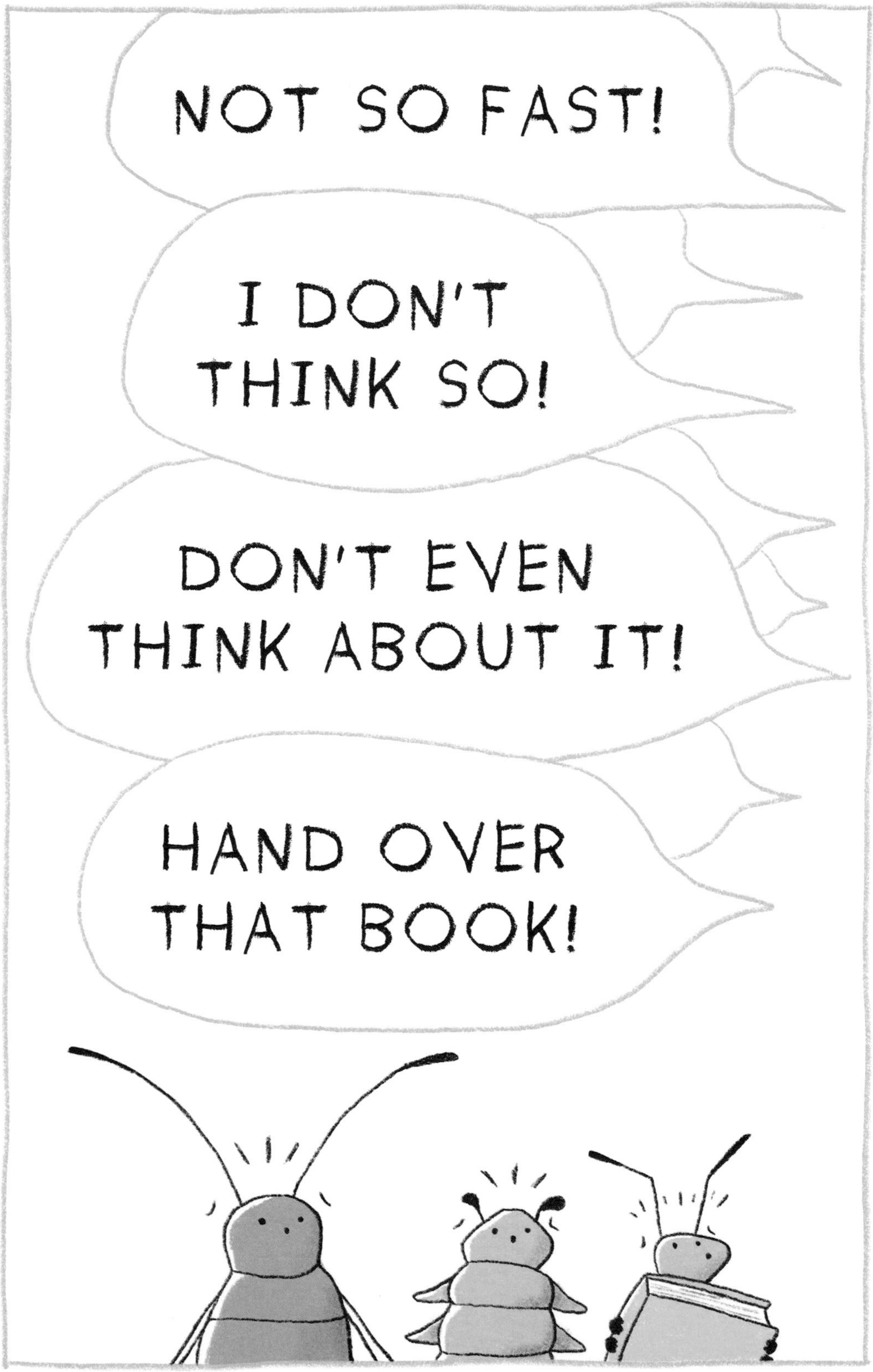
NOT SO FAST!
I DON'T THINK SO!
DON'T EVEN THINK ABOUT IT!
HAND OVER THAT BOOK!

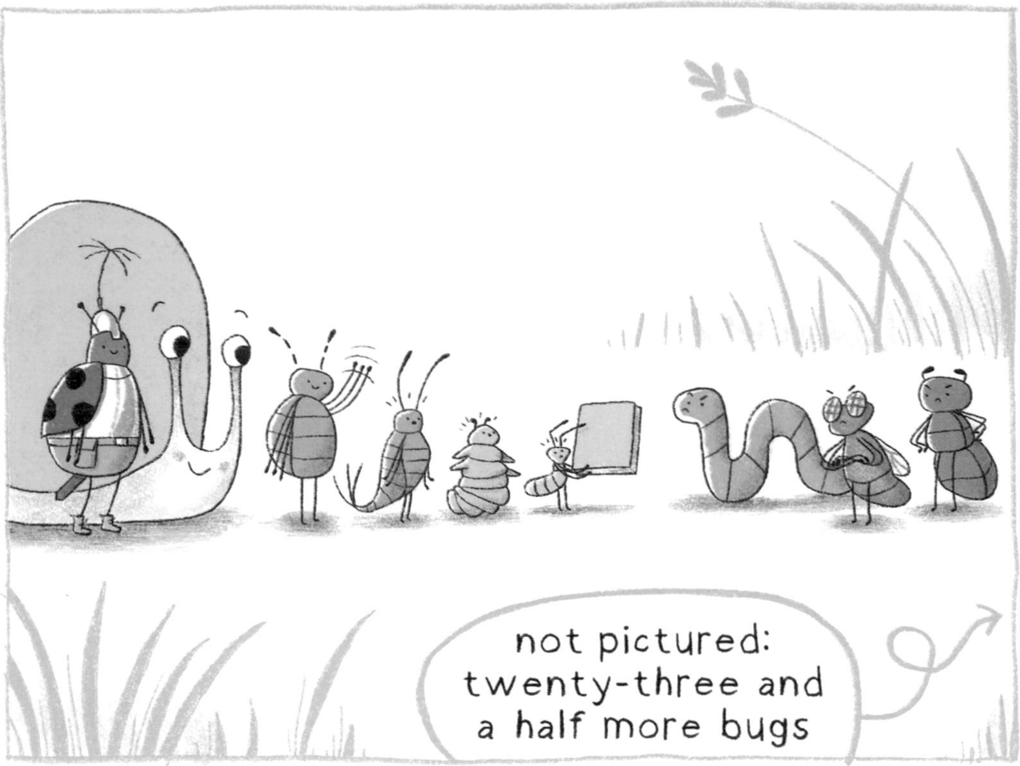
not pictured:
twenty-three and
a half more bugs

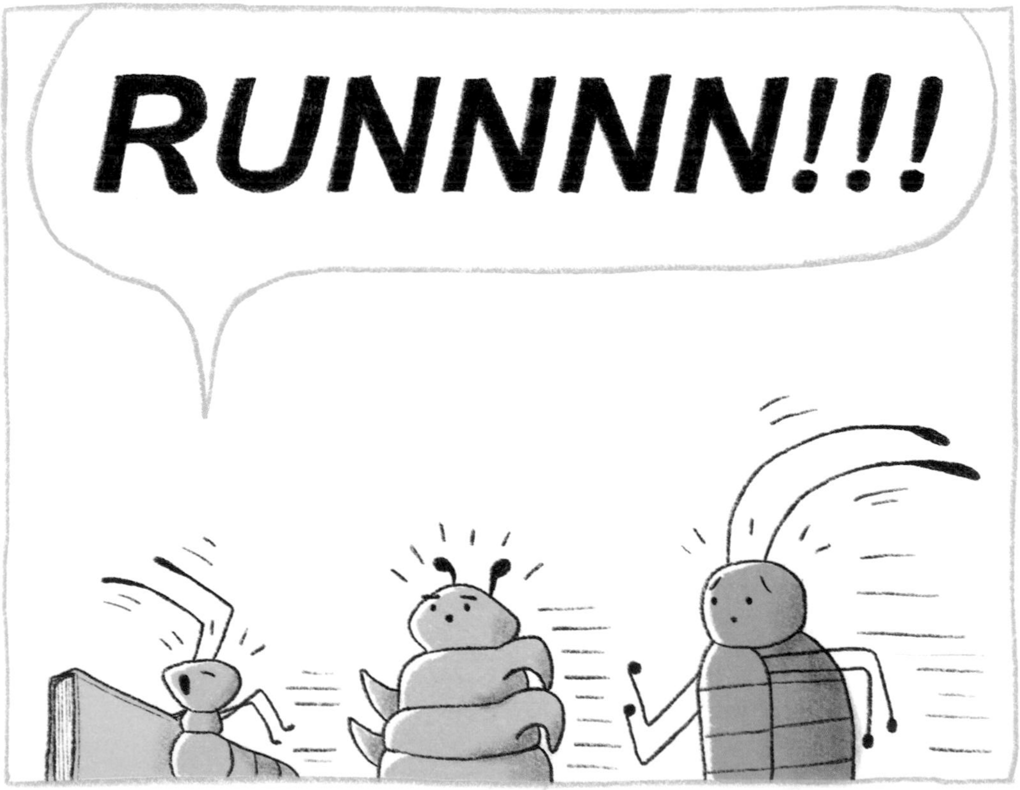
RUNNNN!!!

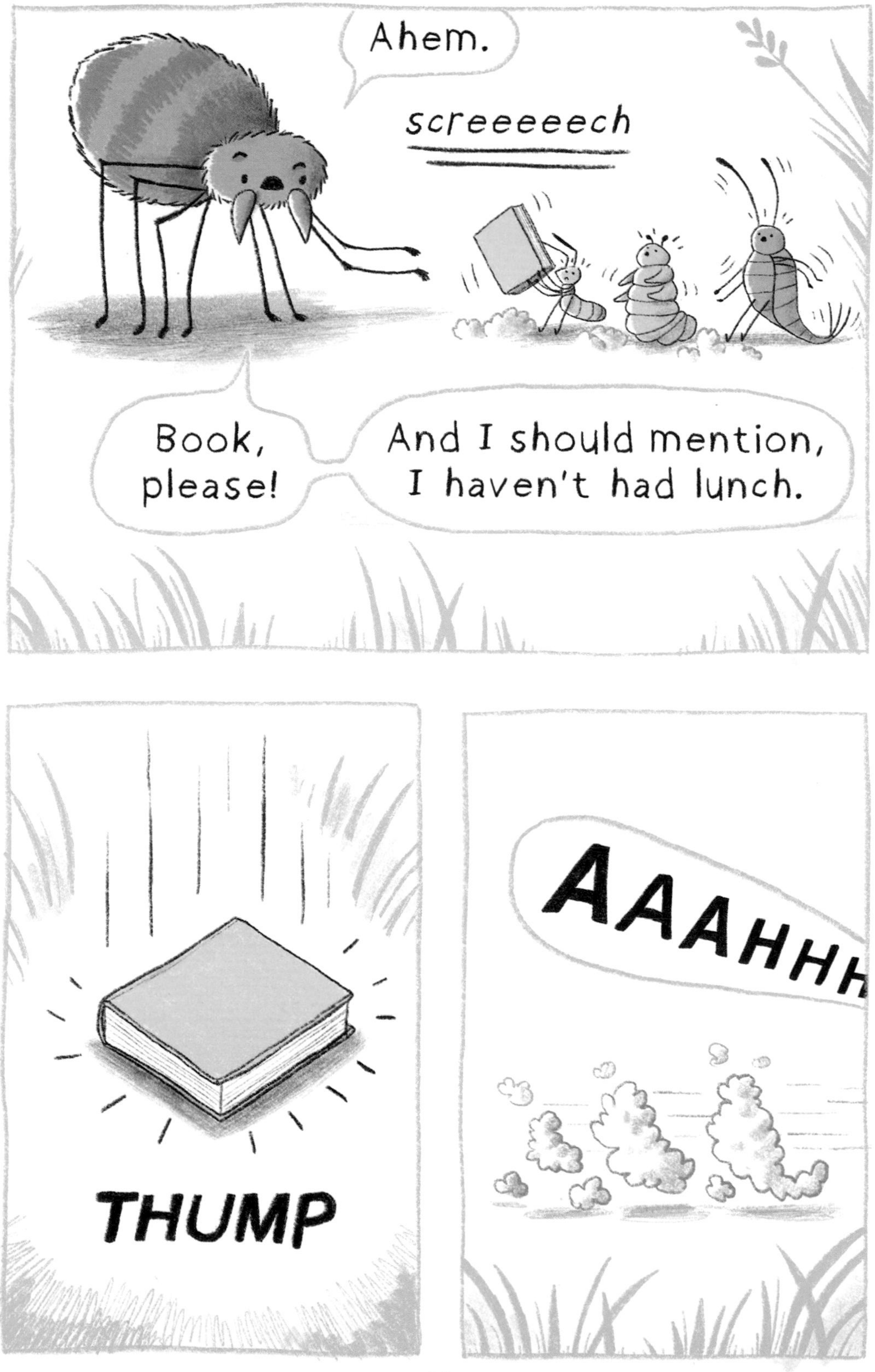
Ahem.
screeeeeech
Book, please!
And I should mention, I haven't had lunch.
THUMP
AAAHHH

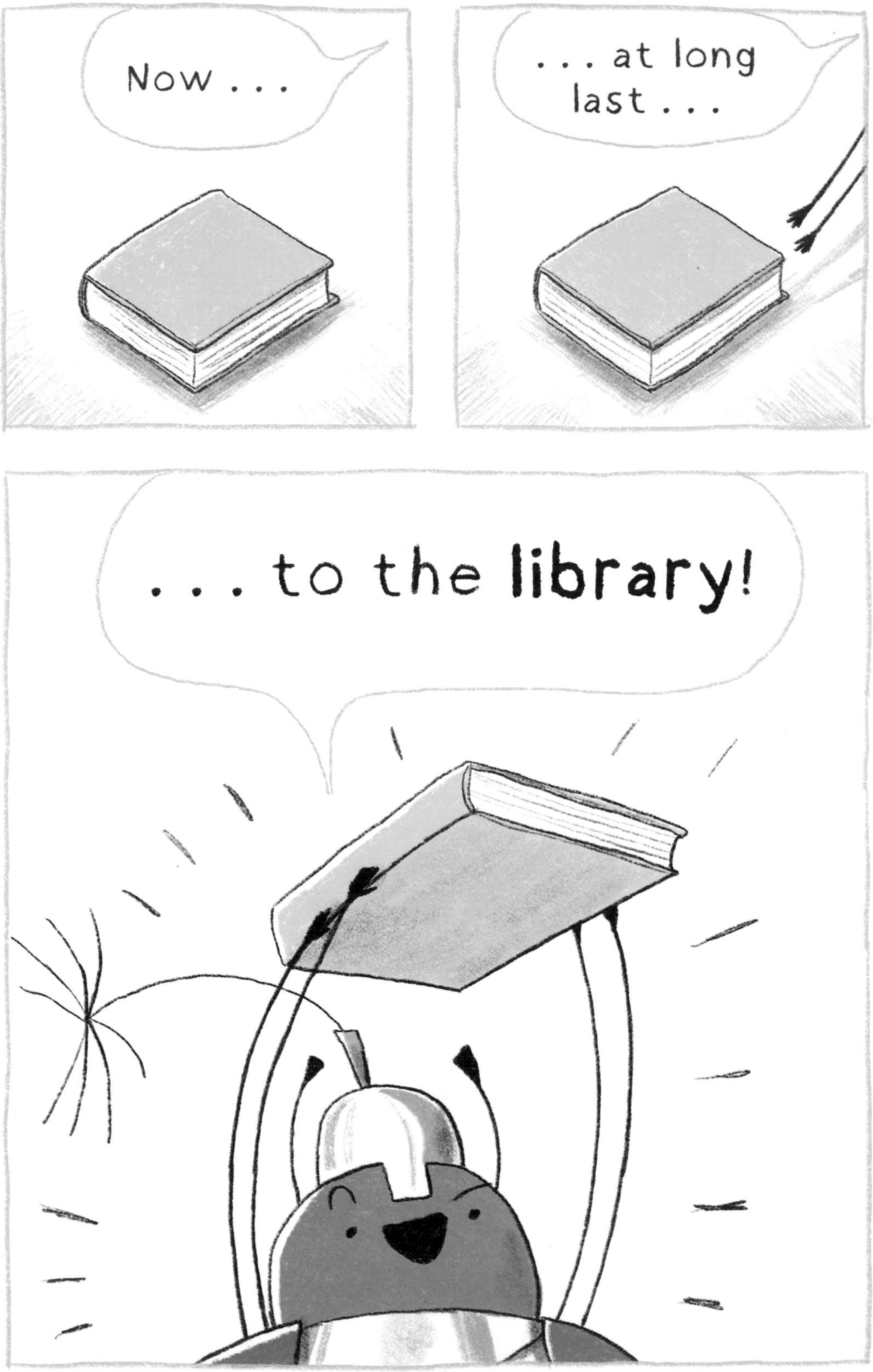
Now . . .
. . . at long last . . .
. . . to the **library**!

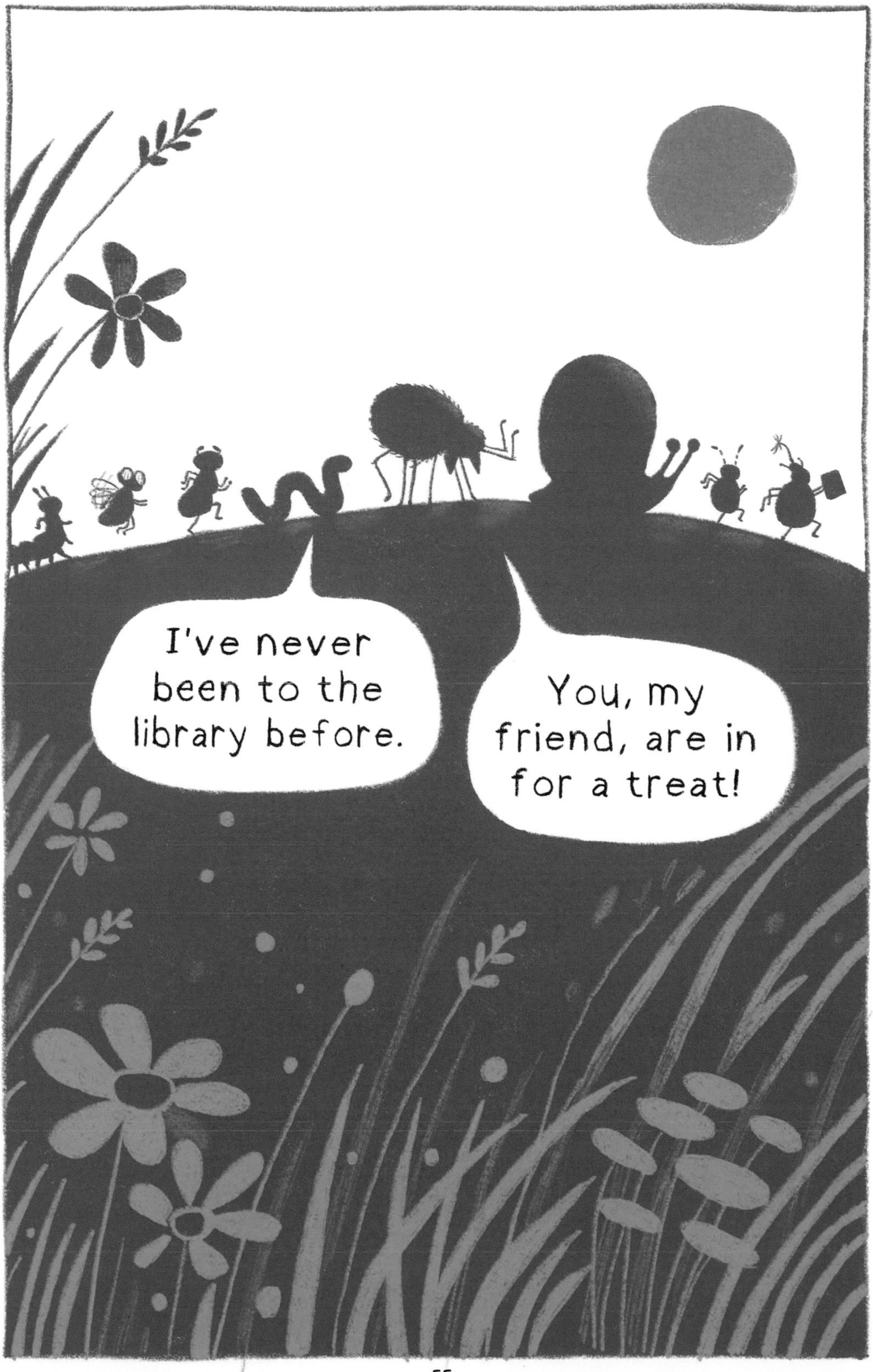

I've never been to the library before.
You, my friend, are in for a treat!

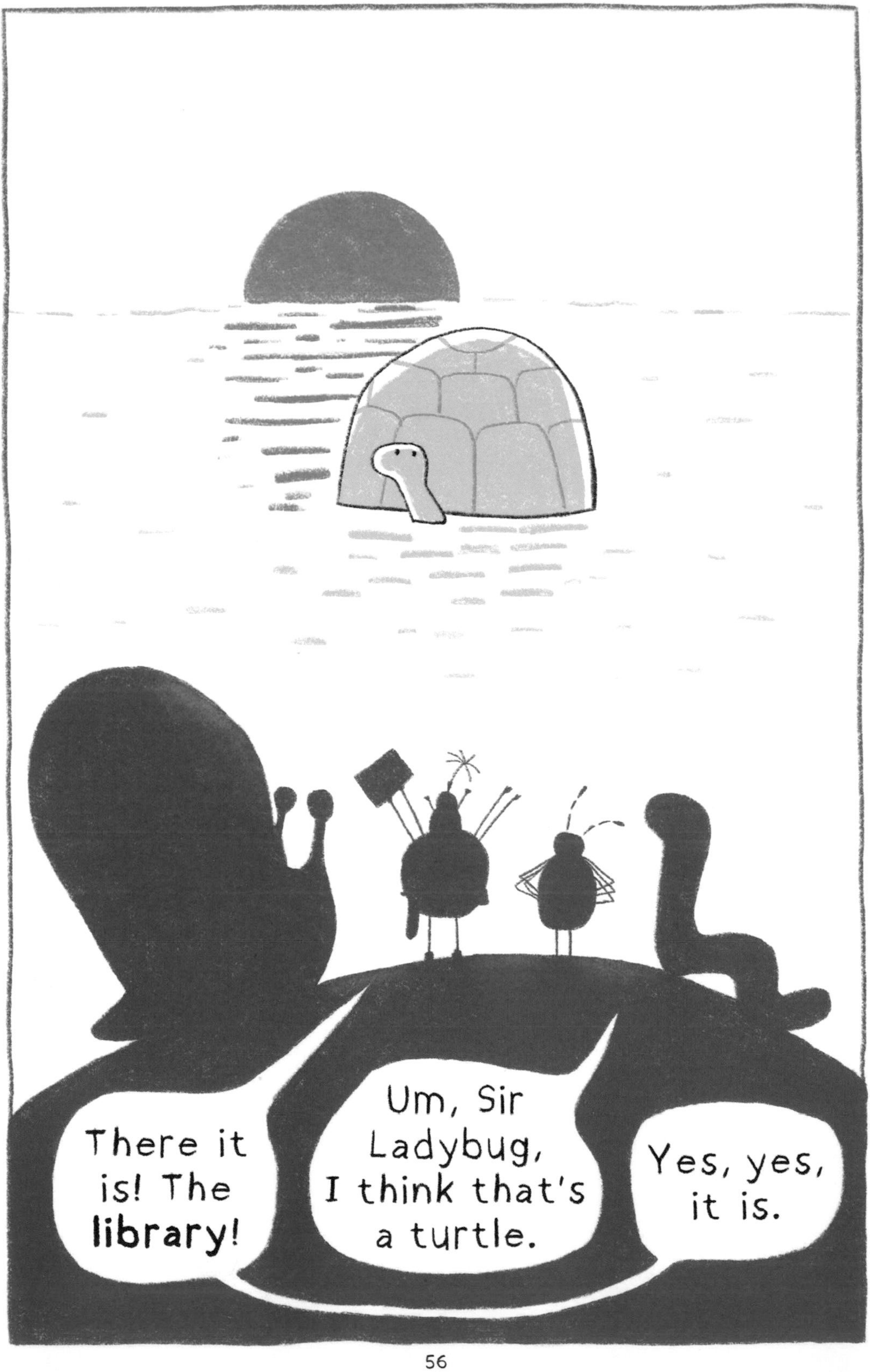
There it is! The **library**!
Um, Sir Ladybug, I think that's a turtle.
Yes, yes, it is.

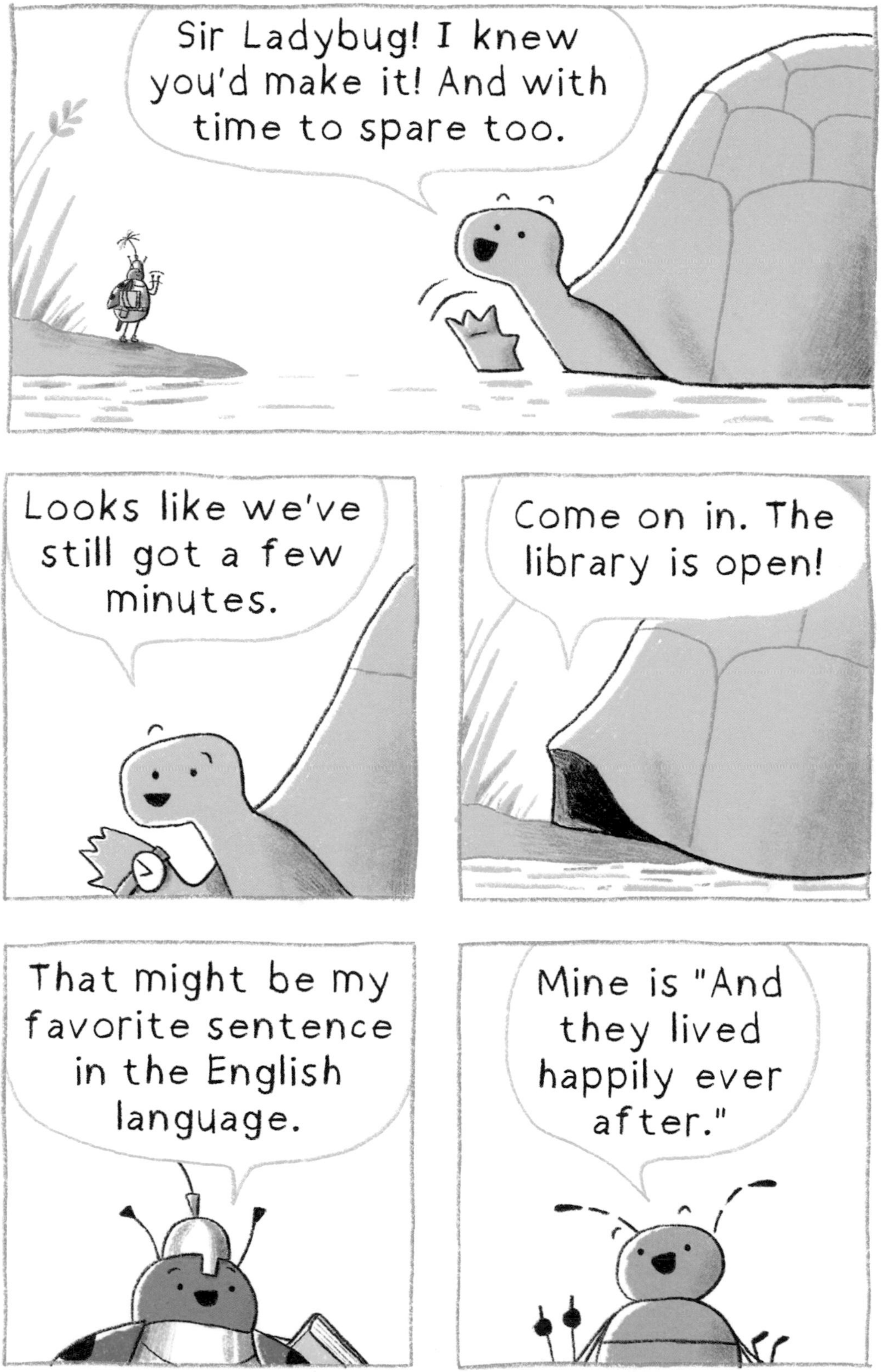
Sir Ladybug! I knew you'd make it! And with time to spare too.
Looks like we've still got a few minutes.
Come on in. The library is open!
That might be my favorite sentence in the English language.
Mine is "And they lived happily ever after."

The Library

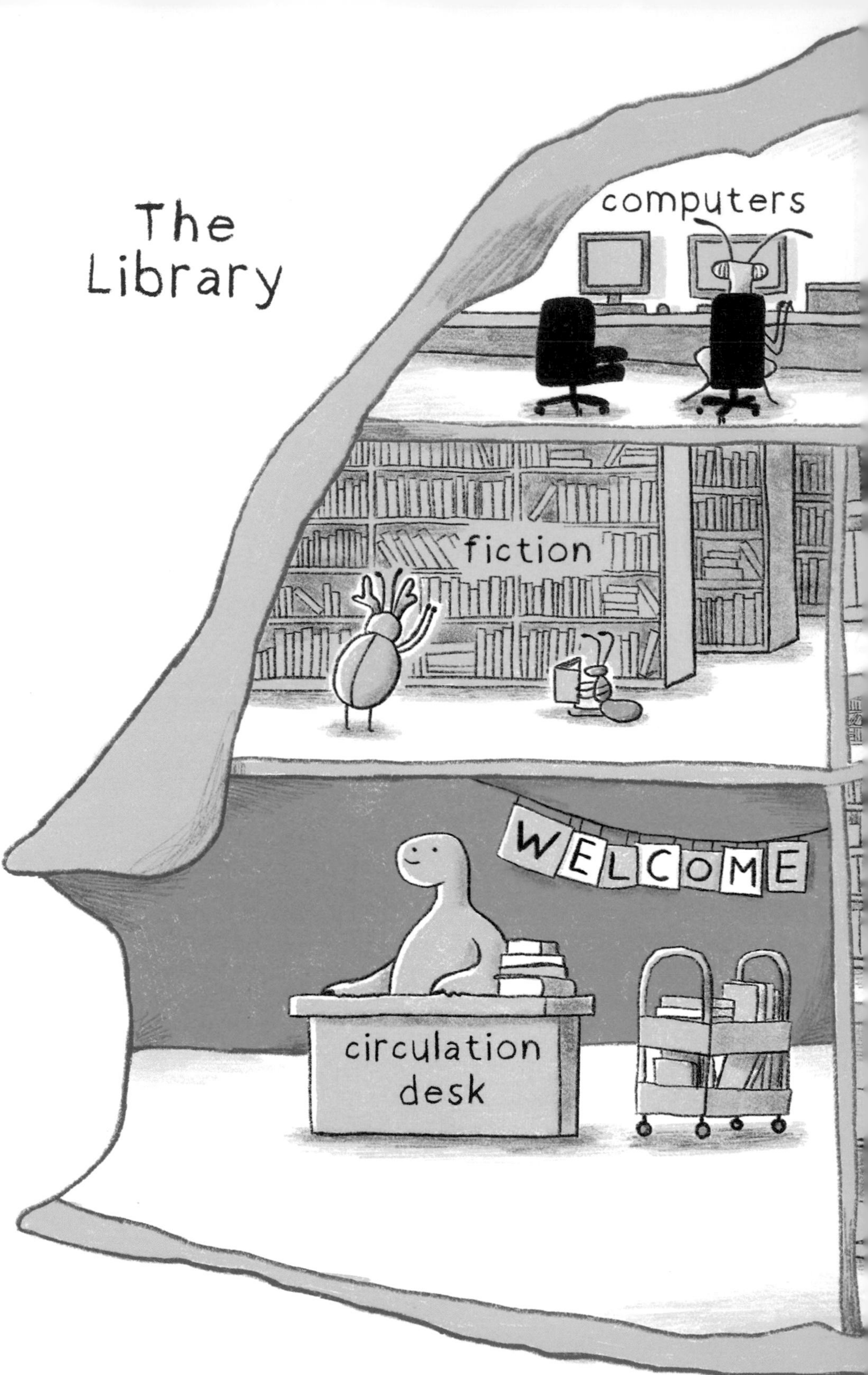
computers
fiction
WELCOME
circulation desk

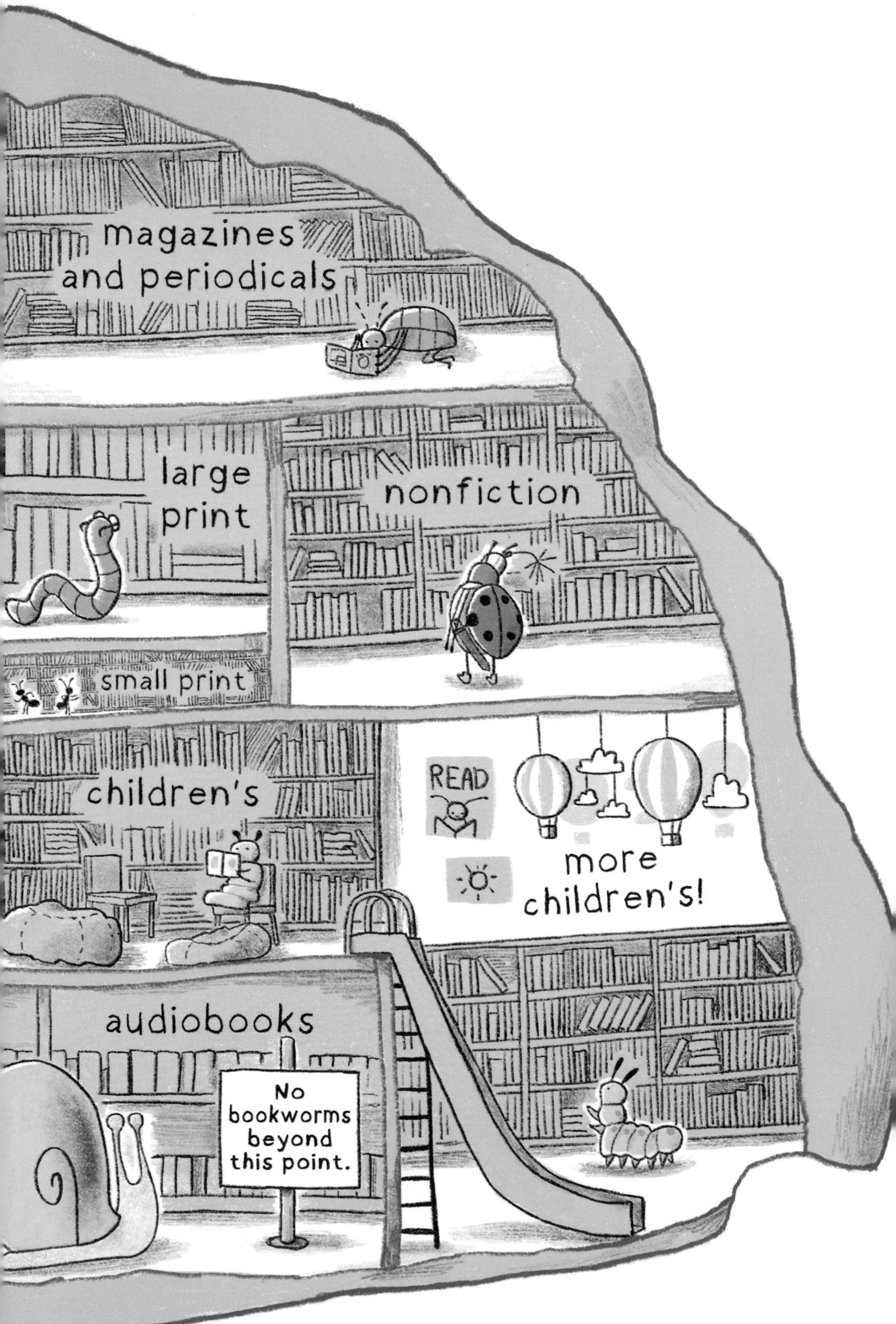
magazines and periodicals
large print
nonfiction
small print
children's
READ
more children's!
audiobooks
No bookworms beyond this point.

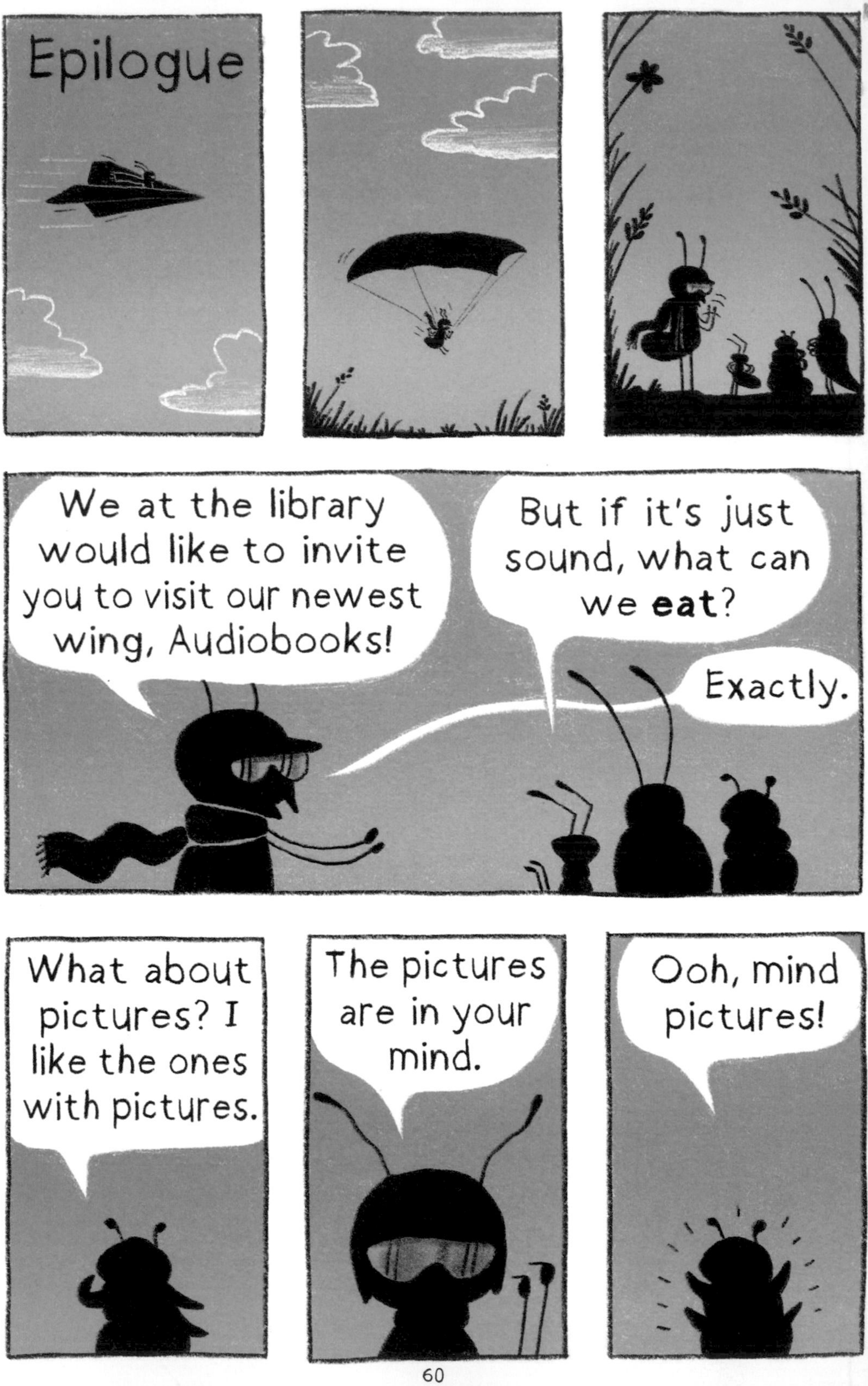
Epilogue
We at the library would like to invite you to visit our newest wing, Audiobooks!
But if it's just sound, what can we **eat**?
Exactly.
What about pictures? I like the ones with pictures.
The pictures are in your mind.
Ooh, mind pictures!